"Exquisite writing...a breath of
fresh air to modern literature."

JASON CRAGER,
AUTHOR OF *UNBRIDLED HUMANITY*

"Great powers of description."

CHRIS GREEN,
AUTHOR OF *NIGHTSWIMMING*

"His ability to tell the tale, with the
minimum of words, is unrivaled."

K. J. WALKER,
AUTHOR ON *BOOKSIE*

"The characters and the truths are
all universal and ageless."

NICHOLAS COCHRAN,
AUTHOR OF *FATAL FLAW*

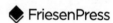
FriesenPress

Suite 300 - 990 Fort St
Victoria, BC, V8V 3K2
Canada

www.friesenpress.com

Copyright © 2021 by Lionel Walfish
Compiled and Edited by Lawrence Lebarge
First Edition — 2021

ISBN
978-1-5255-9611-7 (Hardcover)
978-1-5255-9610-0 (Paperback)
978-1-5255-9612-4 (eBook)

1. Fiction, Short Stories (Single Author)

Distributed to the trade by The Ingram Book Company

Compiled and Edited
by Lawrence Lebarge

Lillian on Sunday

Stories of the Human Heart

LIONEL WALFISH

Special thanks to Julie Penner for her valuable assistance in the preparation of this book.

This book is dedicated to the woman who first shone the light on all of the arts for me,

my mother,

Sarah Auerbach Walfish

Table of Contents

Lillian on Sunday

on Sunday

It was a breathlessly hot Sunday in August, and the noonday sun, a steaming ball of hot orange, hovered over Mount Royal in balloon-like suspension. Even the tall green elms that lined the western slope of the mountain drooped heavy with humidity, offering little relief to those few who sought salvation under their still branches.

Lillian made her way down the winding wooden steps that curved along the mountainside. She paused for a moment to catch her breath. Perhaps it would be best to return to the coolness of her air-conditioned apartment. There was little to do in the way of cleaning up after last night's party. She had awakened early and put the living room in proper order. When she had finished rinsing out the last of the glasses, she knew that she had to get out. The night before had been another pathetic attempt at gathering together the few people she counted as friends, and the evening had ended as did all others: she found herself alone. Achingly alone.

During the week, the days passed quickly for her. Her job as a court stenographer kept Lillian busy enough. When she returned home in the evening—sometimes after eight o'clock—she was happy to soak in a hot tub, eat a light meal, and re-check her text messages.

Sundays, however, were something else.

She continued her descent, circling slowly down the curving path until she reached the iron-barred railing that protected pedestrians from the steep slope on the other side of Pine Avenue. From here, she could see the entire business district of Montreal to the south; and directly beneath her, a staircase leading to a small patch of beautiful park, where a shirtless young man lay sunning himself on the grass.

Even with eyes half-closed, he was aware that she was watching him. He had not noticed her from above, but had seen her look at him when she had descended and entered the park through the iron gates. He was accustomed to these particular kinds of glances. She was older, this one, at least forty, and when he turned over on the flat of his stomach he avoided looking back in her direction.

Lillian walked across the stretch of grass and settled herself down a few feet away from him. He peered up at her from under his folded arms. She was not very pretty.

"It's very hot, isn't it?" Lillian said. She wanted very much to see what she thought she had observed from a distance: the delicately featured face, a brush of soft brown hair over the forehead, and a firm sensuous mouth that perhaps she could coax into a smile. He hadn't heard her. She cleared her throat and made a second attempt.

"This must be one of the warmest days we've had all summer. I used to live in New York City, and the summer heat there was unbearable. Not much better in this city today, though."

He mopped his forehead with the stripped cotton shirt that lay by his side and pushed back the hair that had fallen into his eyes.

"I can't imagine people being able to stay out too long in weather like this," Lillian continued. "Of all days, I had to pick this one to climb the mountain. It really does get to you after awhile, doesn't it?"

He was distracted by a swooping pigeon that appeared from nowhere, landing on the grass and settling beside him.

"Normally I love this type of afternoon," Lillian rambled on. "But sometimes the heat makes me think I'd be much better off having a cold drink in my air-conditioned apartment. What about you? Would you like to have a cool drink with me? I only live over there," she said, pointing south to a high-rise apartment building, just beyond the park.

He smiled shyly, showing fine and even white teeth. *Would this be a repeat of all the others?* he thought. It had always been so difficult for him to make friends. Most of his encounters were of a fleeting nature.

"It's really quite pleasant inside, and there's a beautiful view of the city. Come," she said, standing up and smoothing out her slacks. Deep inside, she heard her voice echo the invitation, and she quickly dismissed a moment of hesitation. He reached for his shirt and, brushing a few blades of grass from it, stood up and started walking slowly beside her.

"Yes, I believe in reality," Lillian said as she reached for a bottle of Perrier from the fridge. "You know, last night I had a small party. Just a few friends. Would you believe that I can honestly say that I really don't know any of them? I mean, not really. At one point after dinner, I looked at each and every one of them, these supposedly good friends of mine, and they were strangers to me. The conversation was so shallow, and nothing was registering. Can you imagine that feeling?"

Lillian handed him a glass, and he took a swallow of the cold liquid, smiling gratefully. The open good looks of his handsome face once again caught at her.

"Sometimes it's so hard to figure out. These people last night. My friends. I think we just spend time using each other." She paused a moment before continuing. "You know, I've been doing all the talking. I mean I really have."

She paused again, waiting for a response.

"Do you think that it was wrong of me to have asked you back here? I mean, I can only imagine what you must be thinking. Honestly, the truth now."

He looked quietly at her and shook his head.

"Well then, you do understand, don't you? That sometimes strangers can be more like friends... and that they can relate better to you than...than the people you number as friends? Oh, I don't know, it all sounds so mixed up, but you know what I mean, don't you?"

He smiled softly and looked down at his knees, balancing the glass between them.

All of sudden she knew, even before he looked back at her, issuing small unintelligible guttural sounds from somewhere deep in his throat. He pointed to his mouth, shaking his head while watching her become undone.

"Oh my God," was all Lillian could manage.

Miraculously her cell phone rang just at that moment, and she excused herself, rushing to answer it in the bedroom.

Moments later, she re-entered the living room. Friends would be arriving at six o'clock. She pointed to her wristwatch, indicating that it was getting late. For some reason she found herself whispering and motioning with her hands. He understood. Whatever thoughts she had entertained in the park had vanished. She wanted him out of her apartment as soon as possible, and he knew that.

When the door closed behind him, Lillian sighed with relief. It was good that there would be company that night. She needed people around her on Sunday. Thank goodness for her friends.

For one brief moment she looked out the window, watching the heat patterns vibrate over the Saint Lawrence River, and for only a fraction of a second, deep within her, she experienced a sharp pang of something lost.

The
Miscreant

Miscreant

Horace Tyler was an insidious, evil man with copious inner bile that seemed to ooze from the very presence of his aura.

At sixty-eight he possessed an impressive, lean, and angular figure. But therein lurked a person of vile self-loathing; a man capable of manifesting calculated harm; a predator always choosing his victims from among those he considered weaker than himself. His motivation was the simple pleasure derived from seeing those close to him squirm uncontrollably, as if speared, harpoon-like, in an unexpected moment; a deer suddenly caught in the headlights of impending doom...

Most of Horace's machinations would take time in the doing; often months, and in some cases even years. But there were exceptions. On the spot devastation was his specialty. An ugly comment, delivered at just the right moment from a darted tongue, could cut, wound, and destroy. Horace's plan in life was to wreak havoc on as many people as he could. It was the only way, he found, that he could assuage some of his unbridled and seething self-hatred.

The bite, when he first felt it, was scarcely more than a slight inconvenient itch; a pin-prick, hardly discernible, beneath a linen shirt sleeve and a heavy layer of grey-black forearm hair. Just a minor irritation, to be sure, in the scheme of things...

It had, however, within the half hour, reddened considerably. As Horace's arm began to swell, a throbbing swirl of tiny bumps lumped together on the inner side of his elbow, following the veins of his arm all the way up to his bony shoulder.

When the first pang of scissor-sharp pain shot through the tall man's chest, he doubled over. When the second dart of hostile intrusion pierced his rib cage, he dropped the frosted martini glass he was holding. He cursed, clutched his heart, and fell face-first into the sweet-smelling primrose and wisteria garden patch that lined the manicured lawns of Mavis Borden-Blatt's summer home.

The black widow spider, undetected by all, scurried out from under Horace Tyler's sleeve cuff, finding its way to a vine-laden trellis nearby.

After the ambulance drove away, those of us who stayed on for a late-night supper of cold meat delicacies and lemon sherbet all agreed that dear Mave gave the best parties ever, 'sans doute'!

Everything

In 1950 I was in the eighth grade of Montreal High School and, having just turned thirteen that autumn, the prospect of getting laid was both a new and frightening one for me. Not that the idea of sexual intercourse hadn't crossed my mind before. It was just that I had never associated myself with any commission of the actual act.

No sooner had I completed one ordeal of symbolically attaining manhood (my bar-mitzvah) than I found myself faced with this new and daunting endeavor. I tried occupying my mind with more constructive thoughts, but my friend Manny was of absolutely no help in the matter.

"Hey, did ya see the boobs on that one?" Manny would ask, leering at the girls in their somber black uniforms on the other side of the high school courtyard. These uniforms were structured in such a pleated way as to conceal whatever special virtues a particular girl might be endowed with;

but somehow Manny always managed to single out the qualities of several black-garbed beauties.

Perhaps it was the advantage of the extra year that Manny had over me, for at thirteen I wasn't really all that knowledgeable. Only a few months prior, I had begun to risk blindness and insanity with the help of my persistent right hand. If at that time I had been told that girls could do it as well, I would have considered it inconceivable, for everyone knew that they didn't have anything down there to do 'it' with.

It was after gym class on Wednesday afternoon that I heard a voice echoing through the basement corridor. "Hey, wait up, will ya?" It was Manny.

I lingered by the stairwell until he caught up, all red faced and excited.

"It's all set up, big guy. She lives on Rachel Street, and all we have to do is call her the night before. Her name is Jenny, and she does it for almost nothing." By this time Manny had caught his breath, and stood there anticipating my reaction.

He had spoken with such enthusiastic conviction that I found myself quickly replying, "That's terrific Manny," and wondering at the same time why little beads of perspiration had suddenly broken out on my forehead.

It was all lined up for a Friday night, a weekend being more sensible than a weeknight, just in case anything went on after ten o'clock. I would doubtless be questioned by my parents if I were late, and there was school the following day. Manny was never questioned, and since he'd been around much more than myself, who hadn't been around at all, I had put complete faith in him.

"This one's really something," he confirmed the afternoon before our scheduled rendezvous, "and she does everything!"

"*Everything*?" I managed to question, not wanting to appear too ignorant in such a worldly matter, and forgetting my concern about the possibility of having failed the Latin exam I had just written. My 'everything' consisted of information memorized from several well-worn pages of Erskine Caldwell's *God's' Little Acre* and Irving Schulman's *The Amboy Dukes*, studied in secret moments on the toilet seat and slipped between the pages of Life Magazine for undetected conveyance. As far as I knew, there was only *one* thing to do, and

I racked my adolescent brain trying to remember something that I might have overlooked.

That Friday evening at dinner I could barely contain myself. The combination of excitement, apprehension, and a bad case of the jitters caused me to choke on each morsel of food that went into my mouth. Fortunately, the conversation revolved around my mother and sister's recent shopping trip to Toronto, so the silence on my part went unnoticed. I had the uncomfortable feeling, however, that my father kept eyeing me with an inquisitive look.

I met Manny as planned, at seven-thirty on the corner of Cote St. Catherine Road and Bellingham Avenue. He was already waiting for me, and greeted me with a broad smile. With masterly pride he reached into his jacket pocket and produced a small flat tin. It snapped open when he pushed at it in a certain way, and with careful fingers he reached for one of several small paper packets inside. He handed it to me and closed the lid, putting the small tin back into his pocket. I started to tear open the printed wrapper in order to discover the contents.

"Not here, stupid!" Manny said, stopping me. "Later, when we get there."

I put the little envelope into the back pocket of my pants, deciding that it would be better not to question the gift. I was too nervous in any event, and was very pleased when the number 29 bus came screeching to a halt in front of us. We boarded the vehicle, put our tickets in the receptacle, and raced each other down the aisle for a window seat.

The ride across town was carried out in silence, broken only by a whistle and a jab from Manny when he spotted a group of girls clustered around a candy store on Park Avenue.

"This is it," he finally said, when the bus came to a stop at the corner of the playground around the lower eastern level of Mount Royal. Several boys were tossing a football, and I had a quick and sudden urge to join them as soon as we disembarked. I followed Manny along a road that severed the park, and soon found myself in a totally unfamiliar area, both geographically and architecturally. The houses along the street seemed to be connected to one another, all very similar in appearance, and each having its own separate staircase leading to doors on different levels of the building. Some of the staircases twisted their ways upwards with series of curving banisters. In my later years I was to learn that this architectural feature was unique to Montreal, but at this particular moment, I was less interested in architecture and more concerned with my own unique problem.

"It's gonna be great, you'll see," Manny said, slapping me on the back and pointing out the house of my impending undoing. "You can go first," he said. "I'll be sloppy seconds this time. I want you to get the works."

The works, I thought. *Was that the same as 'everything?'* I tried to work up as much enthusiasm as my nervous stomach would allow, and at the same time stifle a sudden attack of hiccups. Just the one basic procedure that I had heard and read about had brought on this panic seizure.

"Oh, boy!" I said, trying to react to Manny's excitement while taking long gasps of air into my lungs. At that point I wanted to ask Manny about the small envelope that he had given me, but then I decided on a new strategy. "Manny," I said, "maybe you'd better go first. I mean, you know her and everything, and it might be easier."

"You're not chickening out, are you?" he questioned me, squinting his eyes ever so slightly and searching my face for a telltale sign.

"Of course not," I hiccupped, doubling the pace of my steps so that we were no longer side by side, and I could avoid further interrogation.

It was a four-story building, but, unlike the others on the street, it had no outer staircase.

"Just act natural," Manny said as he pushed open the front door.

We stepped into a small hallway that housed a panel of names and little black buttons. Manny followed the column of names with his finger and, pausing at one of them, pushed the button beside it. We were immediately welcomed by an ear-piercing buzz which instantly cured me of my hiccups, and allowed Manny to push open the inner door. We began our trek up the first long flight of stairs.

"She lives on the third floor," he said. By the time we reached the second landing I felt my knees beginning to knock, and my legs almost buckled underneath me. I stopped for a moment and placed my hand firmly on the wooden banister for support. The sound of a door opening and closing came from the higher landing, and for several moments, the dimly lit stairwell was flooded in a bright orange glare. I thought Manny was a good half-flight ahead of me when suddenly we collided head on, as I continued my upwards climb and he made his way back down, jumping three steps at a time. I didn't have to think twice before bolting after him.

Manny's complexion was almost white. In trying to keep up with him, I found myself almost running. "What's the matter, Manny?" I asked with really grave concern. I felt much steadier now, a curious sense of accomplishment having overtaken me. Manny said nothing, but kept on walking quickly, looking straight ahead. "What happened back there?" I tried asking again.

He was completely silent throughout the bus ride that would take us back home. Whenever I tried to get his attention, he just stared out the window next to his seat. After we got off the bus, Manny finally turned to face me, red-eyed. I could see traces of dried tears on his face. "I saw my father," he said. He was halfway down the street before I could fully comprehend.

I had to wait quite a few more years before I found out about 'everything.' I saw Manny a few times after that incident, but a month or so later I heard that he had quit school and taken a job somewhere. I never saw him again.

Perhaps in those days it was better not to have known about everything.

Mandelbrot

The problem, it seemed, was old Sam Hubsky's snoring. It wasn't as troubling to adjacent apartment neighbors when Mrs. Hubsky was alive. She had devised a concoction that would give her husband a more restful sleep: an old Bulgarian recipe of sheep entrails mixed with exotic herbs, simmered for a fortnight in a large double-boiler.

But now Mrs. Hubsky had passed.

The next-door neighbors on either side, and those across from the Hubsky apartment (in a pre-World War One fabrication located in an older section of Brooklyn, N.Y.), were livid and beside themselves. Sam's snoring was causing them sleepless nights, and banging on the old tenement walls proved useless. Sam Hubsky was almost totally deaf.

One dreary winter morning, as Sam was deciding whether to go out for his morning constitutional to the park, he opened his front door to retrieve his daily newspaper from the hallway. Next to the newspaper, leaning against the wall, was a small food hamper.

Sam picked up the hamper and newspaper and closed the apartment door. Walking back to the kitchen, Sam slowly opened the wooden-handled hamper.

It was full of *mandelbrot*!—his favorite kind, made with whole wheat and filled with nuts. But who could have prepared such delicious cookies for him? Was it Mrs. Gruber, that sweet little lady who lived in the apartment above him? Perhaps it was Rhonda Deutsch, across the hall. She had always been so helpful to his wife with the shopping. Or could it have come from those two nice young men who had recently moved into the apartment next door?

There was no card or letter of identification.

Alas, Sam Hubsky could eat none of the tasty goodies. Having lost all of his teeth a few years back, and not being able to afford a set of the 'Gleaming Cheaters' that he had often seen advertised on his old console television set in the living room, he was resigned to mushy foods and canned soups.

Sam pondered what to do next. He didn't want to appear ungrateful by putting the hamper back in the hallway, and it would seem such a shame to throw all that lovely Mandelbrot in the garbage.

Suddenly he had an idea. He quickly put on his coat, grabbed the hamper and went out. He knew who would enjoy these special treats!

When Sam opened his door the next morning, he reached down for the newspaper and carried it into the kitchen. He poured himself a cup of coffee, sat down and stared blankly at the headline at the bottom of the front page:

HUNDREDS OF BIRDS FOUND
DEAD IN BROOKLYN PARK

A
Massachusetts
Tale

Autumn winds howled relentlessly through the corridors of Wentworth Hall.

The old dormitory had housed youths attending the university for almost a century. When skies turned grey with dark clouds, ushering in the harsh reality of a fast-approaching Massachusetts' winter, the students often complained about the icy cold that found its way into the old structure.

One of the new young inmates of Wentworth, Maurice Beeken, was tiny for his age. At nineteen, when all his peers had long ago shot up in height and girth, Maurice still languished at a mere five feet, weighing only 103 pounds. His dwarfish stature had been the cause of many a joke at his new school, and although he tried to brush off the insensitive remarks, they did in fact hurt him.

October in Blenhem, Massachusetts brought with it, along with swirls of golden wind-blown leaves, a sense of eerie anticipation. A new academic year; teachers, new and old, freshman faces, and of course, the hazing. The town folks had long grown accustomed to this yearly tradition. Older gentry frowned, but put up with the rowdy shenanigans and pranks. Some made sure that their doors were locked, shades drawn and lights turned down.

Maurice knew that he would have to take part in the initiation that was mandatory for a 'new boy.' To refuse would have only added reference to his small stature. What, indeed, had they planned for him? He nervously entered the great dining hall and sat with a group of new students. After a dinner of roast beef and buttered string beans, names were called out in alphabetical order. Maurice was the second name to be called.

"Your assignment, Maurice Beeken, is to go to Blenhem cemetery tonight after midnight. You will bring with you this large metal spike and hammer. When you go through the cemetery gates, you are to turn right and walk about five minutes to the unconsecrated grounds. There you will come upon three large nameless gravestones. Your task is to hammer the spike into the middle stone. In the morning we will check to make sure that you have fulfilled your assignment."

A north-east wind had blown off the Atlantic Ocean that evening, and the temperatures had become nothing less than bone-chilling. Maurice sat in his sparse dormitory room wrapped in two sweaters and a scarf. Reading would help pass the time, and make the midnight hour come quicker. He listened to the clangs of the old church clarion, marking each passing hour.

At the stroke of midnight, he put on an overcoat over his two sweaters, wrapping his long red scarf firmly around his neck and leaving the two ends hanging loosely over the back of his shoulders. He shuddered a little. Maurice had heard stories of Blenheim cemetery. It was an area known for 17th-century witch burials, and he wondered if it were their graves which were found interred in the unconsecrated grounds.

A cloud-filled night did not allow for a moonlit journey. Periodically the howling wind would suddenly die down, and the quiet of the very early morning was interrupted by an occasional hoot owl. Maurice made his way along the one main street leading from the university to Cemetery

Road; about a twenty-minute walk all told. The cold, bitter wind hurt his forehead and cheeks, and he shielded his face with his warm woolen mittens. With each step that he took, he could feel the large hammer thump in his coat pocket against his leg.

When Maurice finally arrived at the cemetery, the gate was slightly ajar. Even without proper lighting, he knew that he could use the iron railing to guide himself to the unconsecrated grounds. He turned right.

The three boulder-like gravestones lay straight ahead, just as he had been told. A slight break in the clouds allowed the moon to reveal their resting place. Reaching into his deep pocket, he grasped the heavy hammer with one hand, and from the other, produced the long metal spike. Just as the moon disappeared again, Maurice lifted the hammer high into the air.

With three heavy blows, he drove the spike deep into the hard rock of the middle stone. Maurice knew that his accomplished feat would serve him in good stead with the other boys. As he turned quickly on his heels to retrace his steps along the railing, something suddenly clutched him from behind, holding him back, making his senses reel. It had caught him firmly by the neck, causing him to gasp for air.

Maurice struggled violently to release himself, but with each effort it pressed itself even tighter around his neck. He thrashed his arms back and forth, trying frantically to release himself from this superhuman grip. Spittle ran down the corners of his mouth, and his eyes bulged out in desperate fear...

After breakfast the following morning, the task master, along with a few other seniors, made their way to the cemetery to check if Maurice had completed his assignment. There they found his lifeless body on the ground, lying against the unmarked gravestone.

Hammered into the stone were both ends of Maurice's long red scarf.

Pernod

Pernod was no ordinary run-of-the-mill house cat. He was as hairless as one could possibly imagine a Peterbald to be. He lived on Bella Vista Drive, in a big beautiful home overlooking the shady hills of Ventura, California. His owners, Dale and Pinky Wasserman, doted on their beloved cat, and treated him in a manner befitting the child they never had.

Pernod's Russian and Siamese heritage was overshadowed by the Balinese and Javanese in his blood, rendering him at least twelve inches taller than the average Peterbald. Standing on long hind legs, his sharp rat-like nails were capable of snatching ornate object d'arts from decorative mahogany curio stands and hiding them in remote corners of the sprawling Ventura home. Equally annoying was his repeated attempts to unfasten his nametag collar, which the Wassermans had gone to great expense to have customized in glittering sliver with aquamarine insets. (Dale Wasserman had insisted the jeweler install a heavy-duty safety clasp on the collar, "just in case.")

The real problem, though, began a week before Pernod celebrated his first birthday, when the Wassermans decided that he was sufficiently trained to accompany either of them during their daily business routines in the workplace.

Pinky Wasserman, a heavy-set, big-boned woman whose comings and goings were always heralded by the noisy clanking of her gold and silver arm bracelets, dealt in high-end real estate. She showed exclusive homes in the Thousand Oaks area of Ventura, California.

Dale Wasserman, diminutive in stature, with three sizable rings on both smallish hands, was the proprietor of Firenze Salon ("Never say shoe store," he was quick to admonish his employees) in downtown Ventura. Manola Blahnik, Jimmy Choo, and Zanotti were on tips of the tongues of the ladies who shopped there.

Pernod's first day at Firenze (which was to be his last) found him gnawing on a Salvatore Ferragamo carry all. "Very bad, Pernod...bad, *bad* cat," Dale Wasserman scolded, wrenching the leather bag's handle from Pernod's steel-like jaws. The cat, suffering instant humiliation, angrily skulked flat-bellied along the thickly piled carpeted floor. He jumped onto a Grecian pedestal, knocking over a hand-painted Crown Staffordshire vase (circa 1920) which miraculously survived its fall.

"First time out of the house nerves," Pinky Wasserman said to her husband later that evening. She rationalized that Pernod was merely cutting his teeth, so to speak, in a new and untried environment. As any parent might believe, this behavior would be outgrown. Perhaps if she took the feline along with her to an open house that she would be conducting later that week, he would learn to act more appropriately.

It was not to be.

"Your cat did *what*?!!" Mamie Hosslager screamed out (actually it was more of an echoing shriek). Pinky was trying to prepare her for what she was about to see upon entering her living room, after the open house had terminated.

Mamie's bay window coverings, superb antique Chenille Portieres (inherited from her grandmother's collection of fine woven German fabrics, circa 1900), had been shredded with knife-like precision; ribbons of flowery remnants lay strewn about the living room floor.

"I had only gone into the kitchen for just the quickest of moments for a glass of water," Pinky explained. "How this could have happened is beyond me. I'll replace the drapes, of course."

Pernod purred preciously, his head poking out from under the vestibule credenza.

"Twenty grand for curtains?" Dale Wasserman hit the roof. "That's insane! Whoever heard of twenty grand for curtains?"

"Well, that's what she said it was," a perplexed Pinky sighed. "And if we don't pay up, I'll lose my roster of clients. She's got a bad tongue, that one."

"Well, that's the end of that cat's frigging fancy feast. Where is he? Where is he?" Dale hollered out twice. "*I'll kill him!*"

But Pernod was nowhere to be seen.

At eight o'clock that same evening, while Pinky and Dale were finishing up their main course of sautéed bay scallops and grilled scampi at La Maisonette, Pinky received a call on her cell phone. She blanched, eyes bulging, and gagged. Dale tried slapping her on the back. All she could do was flail her arms and push him towards the exit of the charmingly decorated eatery.

"Put in on my tab," Dale motioned in pantomime to the Maitre D.

"More than likely, the fire broke out in a void behind the airing cupboard in the kitchen, and the most probable cause was squirrels chewing through cables," Chief Inspector Radwell said. "The rest of the property was destroyed by smoke and heat. I've never seen a place go up so quickly— almost as if gasoline had been poured into every room. Lucky this didn't happen late at night, when you were asleep."

Dale and Pinky knew differently. They exchanged knowing glances as they surveyed the blackened vestiges of their cherished home. After the fire inspector left, the damp and charred ruins were cordoned off with yellow tape, and they were told that it would not be safe to investigate the property for at least three days. There would be rotating security guards on the site every eight hours to keep prowlers and curious neighbors away. With a heavy sigh, Pinky cast her eyes upwards from the debris toward the fading sunset and the silhouetted hills of the Ventura landscape.

———•———

Located on North Vancouver Island, in British Columbia, Canada, there is a marina where wealthy American tourists can dock their luxury yachts and partake of the splendid scenery and endless wildlife trails. Some say the first sighting was in this vicinity. Over the years there have been similar accounts. Through dense thickets of high shrubbery and ancient evergreen, a large rat-like creature has been seen leaping with kangaroo strides; in one instance with a thrashing badger gripped tightly in its steel-like jaws. On another occasion, when seen in the moonlight, something glittery sparkled around its neck.

To this day, no one has been able to identify this apparition. So who is to say if it is...or it isn't.

Wiped
Clean

Babs Nugent mopped her sweaty brow with a work glove from her jean's back pocket.

She descended the ladder that leaned against the large window of the Majestic Food Market and looked up at her work. All the windows gleamed. It was a job well done. One last trip tomorrow, and the arduous task would finally be completed.

Babs made her way to the parking lot and opened the door to her brand-new Cadillac convertible. If she hurried, she would just be able to make a quick clothing change at home, and then meet her husband at his executive golf club on Upper Briar Hill Summit.

As Babs drove quickly out of the parking lot, she glanced over at the windows of the market. They shone brilliantly.

A note on the door read:

THOSE CAUGHT SHOPLIFTING
WILL WASH WINDOWS
EVERYDAY FOR ONE WEEK

All that, she sighed, *just for a jar of pickled gherkins*...

A
Perfect
Day

The Jacquard tie he selected, a light powder blue in perfect silk, milled upon the shores of Lake Como, was an effective mate for his navy buttoned-down shirt. The jeans were stylish to a fault: button fly, five-pocket treatment, and very rugged to the eye. The finishing touch, a dark black blazer with denim detailed interior and accents on the sleeve cuffs, achieved a perfect look. With a single but swift glance at the full-length hallway mirror, he was out the door, walking jauntily into the sun-filled street.

Lunch was to be a special treat. He had not eaten at this particular restaurant before, and the menu, posted daily, had always appealed. He allowed himself to be seated adjacent to the marble fountain. The tranquil sound of falling water was a soothing accompaniment to the soft baroque melodies that wafted from the hidden ceiling speakers.

A simple home-made minestrone started his noon-day repast. He ordered a chilled pinot grigio to accompany tagliolini with shrimp and zucchini in a butter and parmesan sauce, done to perfection. The dessert, sumptuous cherry biscotti, was complete with a latte macchiato. What a deliciously satisfying meal!

When he left the restaurant, it was crisp and cool, a beautiful autumnal afternoon. A matinee of live theatre had been on the agenda for this day for months; a sure to be stunning performance of Hedda Gabler. As he walked a few short blocks to the theatre, he enjoyed the feeling of calm and serenity that overtook him. Yes, he thought, this was going to be a perfect day.

The theatrical experience was more than exhilarating.

The afternoon sun, although setting seasonably earlier, was still warming to his skin as he exited the theatre. Making his way northward from Lincoln Center, along the riverside, he hopped a bus. It carried him by century-old apartment dwellings, Grant's Tomb, Riverside Church, and, far in the distance, the George Washington Bridge, where the view was always spectacular.

He disembarked at 178th Street. The sun was no longer visible, and a cool wind swept up from nowhere, stirring the last of the season's leafy carpet. Eagerly climbing the stairs and reaching the pedestrian passageway of the bridge that loomed high over the darkness of the Hudson River, he disregarded the "Danger" warning signs, and, with one quick leap, was no longer to be seen.

Hilda's
Lament

Lament.

Hilda Huff was livid.

The tranquil environment that she had enjoyed for so many years was to come to an end.

Her neighbor, Bill Raspier, did not seem to mind the impending upset. He had worked as an industrial plant manager up until his retirement back in 1998, and thunderous blasting and ear-piercing screeches had always been part of his working day.

But what about the young couple who had just arrived, Hilda thought, *the couple with the little boy?* Their names had not been posted yet. Surely they hadn't signed a contract knowing their view would be so horrendously obstructed.

In Hilda's mind, City Hall's push for the extended subway plan was outrageous. And adding insult to injury, the subway tracks were going to be *above* ground, making any attempt at having polite

conversation with neighbors impossible. Someone
had to put a stop to this atrocity!

But Hilda knew it was already too late. Two
months ago, the proposal had been ratified and
construction had already begun. The blossoming
lilac and sycamore trees she normally saw at this
time of year were gradually shielded from view as
the cement barriers edged higher and higher.

And what about poor Lottie?

Hilda knew that of all of her neighbors, Lottie
Sears would be the one most devastated. After all,
she had been here the longest.

She had rested in peace since 1861.

W.S.C.

When the sharp edge of the hardcover book slammed down on the small finger of his left hand, it snapped the old brittle bone with a sound reminiscent of a dried twig breaking in two.

He awoke with a start. It was a bad dream, one of those dampened-brow and cold-sweat kinds that left him with racing palpitations.

Slight of stature and bent with age, he sat up in bed, reached for his cane, and padded his way to the bathroom, where he splashed cold water on his face. He then made his way into the tiny kitchen to heat up yesterday's leftover coffee.

He passed the narrow hallway leading to the small parlor, and noticed that an envelope had been slipped under the front door. It was of greeting-card size.

Setting his coffee cup down on a small nest of tables by the door, he propped himself against the hallway wall with the assistance of his cane. He slid his back down until he could grasp the sealed object, then straightened himself up and tore the envelope open. He retrieved his coffee and made his way to the worn settee, switching on the light that hung from a tattered lampshade.

Placing his reading glasses on the perch of his nose, he made out three embossed letters on the front cover of the card: *W. S. C.*

He could not associate the letters with anything in particular. He opened the card and read the invitation. A limousine would arrive, it said, precisely at 2 p.m. the following Sunday, and take him across town to the address inscribed. (There was no telephone number, and an acknowledgement was not requested). The address was familiar, but he could not place it.

W.S.C., he pondered again. There was no one and nothing he could associate those initials with. Perhaps a student whom he had taught long ago?

The last two decades had left him in a drifting complacency, no longer finding comfort in the old

Latin textbooks that lined the dusty bookshelves of his small efficiency apartment. With no family, and the very few friends he had once had all dead or dying, the telephone would rarely ring. He would often, in a somewhat compulsive manner, check to see that the receiver was not off the hook.

He started preparing for the Sunday afternoon event the night before. A black pin-striped suit, which had hung in his closet and remained unworn for decades, still fit, although it drooped somewhat loosely on his concave frame. A white collared shirt, buttoned tightly around his throat and secured with a red-dotted navy tie, completed his appearance.

Sunday afternoon at one o'clock found him sitting by the hallway door, one full hour ahead of the scheduled pick-up time. As he listened to the February winds that whistled through the cracks of the door frame, he went through a list of names of former students: Walter, William, Wade, Wilbur. No, the W.S.C. initials still eluded him.

His reverie was interrupted by the knock on the door that heralded the arrival of his transportation. The car ride was quick, and there was little to see through the darkened windowpanes of the vehicle. Arriving at the destination, he was escorted from the backseat of the sedan by the driver, a heavyset man wearing a woolen cap and dark glasses. The wind blew coldly, and the old man held his thin scarf closer to his face.

The building, a late nineteenth century structure with shuttered casement windows, had not changed much in appearance since he had taught there twenty-five years earlier. The old sign still read:

The Municipal School for Boys
(with its presiding Rector and Vice-Rector).

He was surprised that he had not recognized the address on the invitation, and curious that the building was open on a Sunday.

The driver took his arm and briskly walked him up five stone steps, knocking loudly on the iron-framed oak door. It opened, and the driver departed quickly down the steps. A young man of about twenty-five greeted him. He ushered the old teacher into one of the classrooms, taking his coat, scarf, and cane. "This way, sir," he said, leading him gingerly to an empty desk.

Four other men, ages forty to fifty, were sitting behind the large mahogany teacher's desk at the head of the room, adjacent to the blackboard. They were all wearing dark suits and ties. Each man acknowledged the old teacher's presence with a bow of the head. He didn't recognize any of them.

After about two minutes of silence one of the suited men stood up. He was tall and wiry. "I'm Goldman," he said. "Do you recognize me?" He walked towards the octogenarian. "You strapped me for being 'fat and giggly.' You said my voice sounded more like a girl's than a boy's. I was only twelve! You made me part of the W.S.C."

Another man stood and came forward. "I'm Vishtuba. When I joined your class, my family had just immigrated to this country. You labeled me a displaced person, a 'D.P'. You ridiculed my accent and put me in the W.S.C."

"What about me?" The third man rose. "I'm Robinson—the 'little pansy-boy.' Remember? You used to strap me and make me sit in a corner desk of the classroom with the other members of the W.S.C."

The last man stood. He was the largest of the four, a hulking man with huge muscles. As he pushed his chair back, and began to walk towards the old man, he picked up a heavy book from the teacher's desk. "We were all members of the W.S.C., 'the Weak Sister's Club,'" he said. "It was a name you concocted that followed us throughout high school, making each of our lives a living hell—do you remember? Do you remember that, *Teacher*?"

When the sharp edge of the hardcover book slammed down on the small finger of his left hand, it snapped the old brittle bone, with a sound reminiscent of a dried twig breaking in two...

Epicurean

It's not that she isn't a good cook. Food just doesn't seem to interest her that much.

We've been living together for almost three years now, and you'd think, with all those fancy cookbooks that line the kitchen shelves, there would be a little more variety over the years.

Nope. The same damn thing every day!

At first, I thought, this is the life. Coming from a family that was separated at birth, I began to think that I would never settle down. At a young age, I joined the police force. I was given challenges, and quickly escalated up the ranks. My superiors appreciated me, but I was still lonely. I needed someone special, and if that person could cook, fabulous!

But I guess it wasn't meant to be.

Wait a minute. She's doing something in the kitchen. Here it comes...

"Supper's ready, sweetie!"

"WOOF!"

Fear
of Flying

of Flying

Emma Sloat was upset from the very moment she awakened that morning. Her husband, Morris, had insisted that she keep the doctor's appointment that he had made for her in the afternoon, and just the thought of it made her feel sick to her stomach.

The departure date for their European trip was fast approaching, and Emma's long fear of flying was something that had to be addressed. The idea of being off the ground, suspended in an enclosed compartment, made her ill with anxiety. As a result, their vacations had always been limited to areas that could be reached by car.

But this coming trip was something special. It would be their tenth wedding anniversary, and Morris had planned a trip to Europe, complete with several romantic hideaways.

Hypnotherapy! That's what Morris had told her, insisting that the methods of Doctor Norman Gultz were the only solution. Once and for all, he had said, Emma had to get over this nonsense. Their European departure was only one month away, and three weeks of therapy, at two sessions a week, was all that would be needed to get her on that plane (according to the good doctor).

Sitting in the waiting room of Doctor Gultz's fashionable Fifth Avenue office, Emma nervously chewed on a well-manicured thumbnail. There were no other patients in the waiting room, leading Emma to wonder whether the hour's drive in from Long Island had been worth it. She was checking the clasp of her new diamond brooch, which Morris had given her on her birthday, when the intercom finally buzzed.

Emma jumped up.

The receptionist smiled, stood up slowly from behind her desk, and beckoned Emma to follow her through the large wooden door and into the inner office of Dr. Gultz.

Emma hated the man on sight!

He was a round little troll with blistered lips, bushy hair, and very thick glasses.

"Come in, Mrs. Sloat," Dr. Gultz said, gesturing her toward a leather chair on the opposite side of his desk. Emma sat down, balancing herself tentatively on the edge of the seat.

"No, Mrs. Sloat. You've got to make yourself more comfortable. Sit back, here, let me take your purse. May I call you Emma?" He placed the purse on an adjacent sofa. "We have to begin by making you feel totally comfortable. This is not really hypnosis. You are not going to be put to sleep. You are going to be an active participant in this procedure, and it is your thoughts that are going to be the key."

Emma looked at him dubiously. She noticed that his hands were chubby, showing tufts of matted hair at the wrists. She cringed.

"Please relax, Emma," he persisted. "I will be helping you to quiet your conscious mind, while we focus on your fear...your fear of flying. You will be teaching yourself not to panic. You will think of things that make you feel good. Remember that you are always in complete control. Your thoughts are what create your reality."

The more Emma Sloat looked at the little man, the more he revolted her. It was something about his squinty little eyes that filled her with a complete disgust and--

Brewster! Of course! Dr Gultz was the spitting image of her first husband, Brewster Sprats. She wondered why it hadn't come to her sooner. Suddenly she was transported back to that last evening with Brewster. It was a nightmare she would never forget. He had maligned her terribly, suspecting her of having an affair with his younger business partner (*she had*) and accusing her of marrying him strictly for his money (*she did—it certainly wasn't for his good looks*). She remembered how Brewster had cursed her violently that night, walking out of the house and putting an end to their one-year marriage. Emma would have been relieved, but because of Brewster's team of cunning lawyers, she was left with very little to live on. She was forced to move out of the house and take a job as a nanny, working for the Zerwinsky family across town while living in their basement apartment. On more than one occasion since their divorce, Emma had come across Brewster with his fat new wife at a mid-town shopping mall. She hated him even more. He was shorter and uglier than ever.

Then one day Emma met Morris Sloat. She was at an after-school children's pick-up site, waiting for the Zerwinsky kids, when Morris appeared. He was awaiting his six-year-old grandson, a chore he enjoyed. His daughter-in-law was finishing up with her apprenticeship at a local law firm, and his son was unable to leave his own place of business. For both Emma and Morris, it was love at first sight. After a respectful courtship (Morris' wife had died the year before), Emma accepted his proposal of marriage. Morris was a prominent art dealer, and his profession demanded that he make regular trips to European auction sales. He always urged Emma to accompany him so that he could show her the beauties of Europe, but she would not even consider it. How could she possibly, after what had happened?

The memory of that flight could not be erased. All she had to do was close her eyes and she was once again a little girl with her parents on that plane. They were on a flight to Ohio when the plane suddenly flew into an air-pocket, plunging several hundred feet downwards. Trays of hot and cold beverages and small carry-ons crashed into the arms and hand-protected faces of screaming passengers. It was a horror that she had relived for years.

And now this! Sitting across from a man that reminded her so much of Brewster!

"Now, close your eyes, Emma," Dr. Gultz continued, "and think pleasant thoughts. Something you are comfortable with. Nothing is going to harm you."

But all Emma could think of was Brewster Spats, who *had* harmed her. He was the man who had tried to destroy her. "You're boarding a plane, Emma. It's a beautiful day out. The sun is warm on your skin. Perhaps you're hearing soft classical music…"

Emma was on the tarmac, lined up to enter the plane. She heard the happy chatter of fellow passengers. Suddenly, just ahead of her, she saw the squat figure of Brewster Spats boarding the plane. She tried to put the thought of her ex-husband out of her mind, but every time she opened her eyes and looked at the bloated little doctor sitting across from her, Brewster's image appeared closer and closer. *She saw Brewster taking a window seat, and when she boarded the plane herself, the only available seat was the one right next to him.* Right away Emma knew that she had to imagine herself off that plane. She just had to. And very quickly!

"We'll have a more successful session next time, Emma," Dr. Gultz said. "The first time can be a bit trying."

Emma tried to shake off the horrible thoughts that she had been having. She wouldn't take the doctor's repugnant little hand, even when he extended it a second time.

"Our next appointment will have to be later next week" Dr. Gultz said. "I'm taking the late-night flight to Miami this evening, and I won't be back for a week. Just check with my receptionist on your way out. And always remember, Emma, your thoughts create your reality."

Emma knew that she was not going to go back to Dr. Gultz. She was never going to board an aircraft again in her life. The image of her despicable first husband sitting beside her on a plane had now *doubled* her fear of flying. She would convince Morris that they could have a wonderful tenth wedding anniversary without having to board a plane.

Emma was feeling better already. She would tell Morris that the afternoon went well, but really, she didn't want to go back. Perhaps a leisurely drive to the Catskills, would make a nice tenth anniversary holiday.

Early the next morning, on his way to get the newspaper that had just been delivered on the doorstep, Morris was still hoping that Emma might change her mind and give Doctor Gultz one more chance. Their next-door neighbor, Harry Feldstein, was standing in front of his own doorway, looking down at the Daily Herald. He looked up at Morris, shook his head and said, "Terrible about that late night flight to Miami, huh?"

Don't Ask

When Mike first laid his eyes on her, he knew it. He just couldn't resist the way she tilted her head to the left each time she laughed, appreciating his quirky sense of humor.

Mike was a simple man of no great monetary means, but hard-working and reliable. Mary was a practicing nurse at a local hospital, showering love and care on each patient that came within her contact. They met by chance in the hospital cafeteria. She was having lunch and Mike, an electrician by trade, was replacing the light fixtures over the food displays.

For their first date, he picked her up in his truck in front of her three-story apartment building and took her to his favorite intimately-lit Italian restaurant in lower Manhattan. It was on that night, sipping red wine before dinner, that he knew it for sure. She was the only woman for him.

Just two weeks later he whispered something in her ear, his cheek brushing hers. She smiled. Reaching into his jacket pocket he produced a tiny velvet box, took out a small ring, and placed it on the fourth finger of her left hand.

"There's something that I must tell you," she said quietly, touching his right hand. "I'm two months pregnant."

"I don't care," he said, kissing her on the cheek.

"But I think you should know. The father is—"

"No, I don't need to know. I love you. I'll always love you. We'll raise the child as our own."

In the suburban community of Croton-On-Hudson on the shores of the Hudson River, the couple purchased a small dream home. It surprisingly featured a nursery room decorated in rose and blue wall accents.

Seven months later, little Erik arrived.

When they had first been told of the prognosis during the second trimester, Mary had negated any possibility of an abortion. After all, she was a nurse, and could easily adapt to the challenges of her son's special needs. Mike was in total agreement. He promised he would take on double shifts to make up for Mary's loss of nursing income. Both of them decided that an institution would never do what they could for their son.

Ten years later, Erik was too heavy and too large for Mary to lift in and out of the hand crafted crib that Mike had built for him on his eighth birthday. Each night she would have to wait for Mike, who would only come home well after midnight. Together they would change Erik's diaper.

One night, Mike arrived home worn and tired. The construction business had slowed down considerably, more so in the dead of winter, and he was taking on as many out- of- town jobs as he could. He headed straight for bed.

As he lay looking up at the ceiling, he could hear Mary reciting nursery rhymes to that 'thing' in the nursery. When she finally opened the bedroom door, he blurted out, "I need help. I'm working sixteen hours a day, six days a week. I can't manage it any more. I need help! Who is he??"

"Who?"

"The father. Who is the father? He needs to contribute!"

Mary's face softened and, taking Mike's hand in hers, she spoke gently, trying not to be disturbed by the sharp goose honking sounds coming from the nursery.

"You didn't want to know then," she said. "And you're not going to know now."

Standing Ovation

By 5:45 p.m., Stanley Webb was exhausted. It was Saturday afternoon, and the week couldn't end fast enough.

Shifting his weight from one sore foot to another at Bailey's Shoe Store, he awaited what hopefully would be the final customer of the day. The store's owner, Mr. Charles Bailey (formerly Beliovsky), would not allow Stanley to sit while awaiting any late afternoon shoppers that might walk through the door.

"You must always give the impression, Stanley," Mr. Bailey said, in his heavy Eastern European accent, "that you appear anxious to be accommodating whenever a customer walks in, and *not* be seen getting up from a seated position. Do you understand me, Stanley?"

"But I have been standing, Mr. Bailey!" Stanley was quick to respond.

"Well, Stanley," Mr. Bailey said, "It looked very much to me like you were *going* to sit down."

Stanley had gone from job to job, simply making ends meet. Now, at the age of sixty-seven, he survived on a meager government pension and the shoe store's minimum wage.

When Stanley finally arrived home that evening, he collapsed into an old, overstuffed Queen Anne winged chair, a gift from a distant aunt who had long ago passed. The chair took up a large portion of his tiny bed-sitting room. The pillowed back and arms engulfed his tired body, and he slowly drifted off to sleep.

———•———

Lilly Van Doren fastened her long flowing blond hair into a bun, holding it securely in place with an enormous crystal hairpin. Sitting in the dressing room of the Starlet Night Club, she admired her reflection in the cracked oval mirror adjacent to the dressing table. She leaned forward, making sure that the right amount of cleavage was pushed up and visible. She stood, shifted her body in the tight-fitting red dress, and smiled with approval at the sparkling sequins. It would be another successful Saturday night, filled with hoots and hollers from the mostly male club-goers.

Lilly was magnificent to behold, and with the skillful application of thick pancake make-up, she had erased every sag and wrinkle from her ageing face and neck in a miraculous effect. She pursed her red lips, blowing kisses at the image that shone back.

Lilly acknowledged the knock on the door, indicating that she was on, and strutted onto the stage, miming the words to an old Ella Fitzgerald jazz hit that echoed through crackly speakers. She beamed as the whistles and cheers filled the room. In song after song, Lilly's gyrations brought the audience to its feet.

What a night it was!

———•———

Stanley arrived home after 2 a.m. on Sunday morning. Without removing the wig, or scrubbing off the heavily applied make-up, he collapsed into the overstuffed Queen Anne chair.

It felt so good to be off his feet.

Something Missing

"Did you ever feel as though a part of you is missing?" Elsie asked in an abstract manner.

"What do you mean?" Dr. Glassner responded, adjusting her horn-rimmed glasses.

"I mean that sometimes, I feel unfinished. I can't quite explain it."

"How long have you been feeling this way?"

"I don't really know. I think I've always felt it. And the feeling became stronger after I left West Virginia, after I married Terrance. My mother was against our coming to Chicago, but Terrance knew that in order to carve out a future, he was not going to make it in Farmington."

"Maybe you're missing your parents?" the doctor suggested.

"No, I don't think it's that. I speak to my mom twice a week. My dad's been gone since I was small. I see my mom every summer for three weeks. The kids used to come with me."

"How's family life coming along?"

"Fine," Elsie said. "The twins are away in college now, and quite self-sufficient, as well as being inseparable. Terrance is doing well at Spivack and Johnson. There's talk about making him a partner. Everything's fine. It's just...this nagging feeling of 'something missing'."

"Do you think it might be the twins?"

"You mean, 'empty nest syndrome'? Oh, no. As I said, I've had this feeling for years...all my life, really."

"Well," Dr. Glassner said, glancing at her wrist-watch. "This is certainly something that we can explore in future sessions." The doctor stood up from her chair and offered Elsie her hand. "We'll talk more about this next week. I don't think it's anything serious."

When Elsie called her mother that night, the conversation drifted to Elsie's childhood.

"But you were a gorgeous child," her mother said. "Everyone loved you!"

"Mom, I'm sure something happened to me, but I don't know what it was. Sometimes I go about feeling that something's just not right. I feel so lonely, with this deep emptiness inside me, even when I'm with Terrance. Did anything happen to me?"

"Nothing happened to you, dear. You were a happy child."

"Yes, I know Mom, but why am I feeling this way? And why so much now?"

Her mother hesitated. "You must be missing the twins. I'm sure that—"

"I'm not missing the twins. Mom, what happened in my childhood?"

"Elsie," her mother said. "Maybe you should come home for a few days."

"Chicago is my home, Mom! Why can't you talk about this to me on the phone now?"

"Can you leave Terrance for a weekend?"

"What is it, Mom?"

"Come home, dear."

A few nights later, Elsie was sitting across from her mother in the old farm-style home that her parents had bought shortly after their marriage. Both women looked intently at each other.

"I was giving birth," her mother said, her eyes glazing over. "Old Mrs. Brenner was assisting me in the bedroom. Your father was sitting here in the kitchen, awaiting any instructions that might be given him. Then there was that terrible explosion that literally rocked the house. The earth trembled around us. Dishes fell from the plate rail in the dining room, crashing and breaking on the floor. It was early morning, about 5 o'clock—"

"Yes," Elsie interrupted, "that terrible coal mining explosion, not far from here. I heard all those awful stories when I was growing up. It happened the day I was born."

"There were two of you," her mother continued. "You came first. Then a boy...he didn't come out

118

right. He was all twisted and ugly, with the baby cord wrapped around his neck."

Elsie gasped.

"Your father was beside himself. He knew he had to get to the mine. After Mrs. Brenner cut the cord, I begged him to take the baby to the hospital, that maybe we could save him. But he said there wasn't time. He had to get to his friends at the mine."

"What did he do?"

"He took him, wrapped him in his leather jacket, and then he..." Elsie's mother stood up and went to the window and looked out into the darkness. "Mrs. Brenner watched it all from the window... said she wouldn't tell a soul."

"What happened?" Elsie asked.

"Elsie, you have to understand...your father saved many a man's life that day. Why, without him they say—"

"Mom, tell me! What did Dad do with my brother?"

"In the well...in the back field...your father put your brother in the well. A few days later he sealed it up. Told everyone it had gone dry. It was too dangerous, he said...for little children to be playing around an empty well."

After a moment of silence, Elsie stood up and walked over to her mother. She put her arms around her.

"Little children..." Elsie repeated, and gently hugged her.

Pretty
Things

It all seemed so strange, Lillie Mathilde thought as she mused upon the passage of time. It was as if she had drifted from one plateau to another without skipping a beat. Her love of pretty things had often found her taking this route along the network of curving tunnels that made up the Paris Metropolitan. She loved to explore little shops and boutiques, in out-of-the-way places, all connected by this serpentine artery buried deep beneath the city.

How detached she had become over the years. Almost an undoing, as it were.

She remembered the first time she had boarded the new underground trains, grasping tightly at her father's sleeve. She was five years old. Papa had taken her from their home in Le Touquet by land train to Paris, to stay overnight at a small auberge. Early the next morning they had both marveled at the sight of the brand-new Metropolitan line, and the silver quick speed with which it carried them to the Great Exposition. The rest of that day had faded from memory, but she still had the lovely porcelain doll that Papa bought for her at the Grand Belgian Pavilion.

As the train rumbled on, she thought of her life as a child in Le Touquet. It was a charmed life, as they say. Her father, the school administrator, intense and noble, was never to be seen without his waist-coat, jacket, and gold pocket-watch. Her mother, the proprietress of a small baked goods shop that had been her grandmother's many years prior, was always in her crisply pleated white apron, save for Sundays and church-going. Deliciously aromatic smells would waft from the bread and pastry ovens, reaching parts of the wind-swept coastal dunes where holiday makers were arriving from all over France and England, filling up palatial hotels that seemed to spring up yearly along the rugged coastline. Yes, her life in Le Touquet had been heaven on earth.

Lillie Mathilde sat up abruptly when station Liege approached. She well remembered how, as a young teenager, this metro stop had been called 'Berlin.' So many things changed abruptly after 1914. She had become beautiful, entering her twenties. The British soldiers, who occupied the grand coastal hotels of Le Touquet, often commented on her tiny waist and ample bosom. They gave her pretty things.

Years flew by, and times became difficult for her after the First World War. Both of Lillie Mathilde's parents had passed, and being neither baker nor scholar, she found herself welcoming the help of older gentlemen, who also gave her pretty things. Now, at age forty-three, she resided in Paris in a small boarding house near Montmartre. She no longer possessed the slender figure of yester-year. Her body had thickened, and her hair, still colored with henna, was no longer luxurious. But although Lillie Mathilde had become a large woman, she was always neatly dressed and coiffed, her black suit perfectly pressed, her white blouse stiffly starched and open at the neckline, to show a single strand of pearls. The small inheritance that she had received from her parents still allowed her some pride of appearance.

Lifting herself off the wooden metro seat bench with a sigh, she exited the train and made her way through the steel-framed door that would lead her to the cobblestone street above. It was May 28th, 1940, and the headlines in all the news-papers prophesied doom for France. Belgium had surrendered to the Germans, and it was just a matter of weeks, perhaps days, before Paris would fall.

Lillie Mathilde pondered this as she walked the short distance to the old stone building that housed her tiny room. As she climbed the crooked steps, she paused for breath. Soldiers would soon be filling the city of Paris. Maybe, just maybe, she thought, she would once again have pretty things.

Swamped

Dr. George Rufus was stunned.

During the course of a two-month period, he had lost almost every one of his patients. The new office that had opened two floors beneath him was draining him of his entire roster of clients. Even Myra Klutzinger, whose ten ingrown toenails were so deep that she needed special padding between each bloated infected toe, no longer visited him. How could all of this have happened, and *so quickly?*

In the basement of the medical building, in the early hours of the morning, four young women sat at a table, their hands working furiously. They knew that their boss, that handsome young podiatrist who had just moved into the office on the second floor, was anxiously awaiting the completion of their work. At any moment now he would arrive and snap up another list of names, addresses and telephone numbers of prospective patients who would bombard his office later on that week. And who wouldn't, especially since the good doctor was charging everyone fifty percent less than his competitor?

As the sun rose, the women continued working away at a fever pitch, meticulously gluing together hundreds of pieces of shredded paper—copies of bills with addresses, duplicate memos, etc.—all gathered from large black plastic bags left by the medical building for the late-night garbage pick- up.

The new doctor would be swamped!

An
Ill Wind

THE WITCH

Everything was just about as perfect as it could be. The silverware, placed carefully on the red and black linen place-mats, gleamed luxuriously under the overhanging stainless steel and glass fixtures. The crystal wine goblets sparkled, throwing fiery patterns in all directions of the dining area.

Edith Barrington surveyed her apartment with glowing admiration. Every piece of furniture, so carefully chosen, was a sheer delight to the eye. Each article softly complimented the other, from the moss-green antique velvet sofa, with its huge overstuffed pillows, to the Jacobean coffee tables and the white faux bearskin rug. Walking over to the huge windows that encompassed the length of her apartment, she gazed out at the city twinkling far below and breathed a deep sigh of self-satisfaction.

Edith Barrington was self-made, beautiful, and envied.

She smoothed her long black hair away from her forehead and glanced at her profile in the large oval mirror that hung in the floral-wallpapered hallway. She gently touched her face, tracing a cheekbone with the index finger of a long-tapered hand. Her porcelain-like skin responded, bringing a light flush to its texture.

Suddenly, the automatic buzzer sounded from the kitchen stove, interrupting Edith's semi-trance and letting her know that the toasted French rolls were ready.

Edith had taken great pains with this particular dinner. The moules mariniere had required particular preparation. She had spent the better part of an hour scrubbing the mussels with a wire brush, steaming them in garlic and wine, and then straining the liquid through a linen napkin. The Romaine salad was much easier to prepare, and she smiled as she checked the vinaigrette sauce, knowing that it was sure to please. The chocolate mousse was being chilled in the freezer, and all that was left for her to do was to bathe and dress.

Before heading to her marble bathroom, she decided to sample one moule, and then another.

Yes, they were perfect. How she loved to feel these succulent little delicacies slide deliciously down her long throat. She couldn't resist popping one more into her eagerly waiting mouth.

As Edith soaped herself in the sunken marble bathtub, she lifted one leg high in the air, remembering how she had instructed her favorite model, Babette, to raise her leg for the Floral Bath Oil account at the agency. Edith watched the soap cascade slowly down her own silken skin. Surely her own leg, she thought, was even lovelier.

Max Benson: short, fat and balding. Edith chuckled to herself as she thought of how he had once referred to her as 'Edith the Iceberg', or so she had been told. This was why she had decided to forgo a regular cold business lunch and invite Max, president of Taylor and Benson, to her home for a quiet dinner, cocktails, and wine. Even after his first martini, she imagined, Max would remain uneasy. The second would do nothing to relax him. She pictured him clumsily knocking over his martini glass while reaching for a crudité. A small stuffed green olive would roll along the glass coffee table, plopping onto the thick hair of the white bearskin rug beneath him.

How awkward he would feel.

The moules mariniere would be next. She would set the steaming silver tureen down on the dining room table, watching him stare in horror at the shells. Daintily, she would lift a shell from her bowl with a spoon very slowly, so that he could try to follow her example. Max would make a fumbled attempt, only to have the moule slip from his grasp, landing back in the bowl with a crash, splattering the crystal and silverware with hot yellowish broth.

How embarrassing it would be for poor Max!

Edith toweled herself dry in front of the reflecting floor-to-ceiling mirrors and moved to her dressing room. She decided on a long white crepe hostess outfit, halter-topped, and cinched at the waist with a huge rhinestone-studded belt at least four inches wide. The silk felt good against her freshly-scented skin, and she was proud of the fact that she did not require a bra.

Max was due to arrive in ten minutes, which gave Edith just enough time to quickly review the details of the contract she had prepared for him to sign, a contract that was to give her agency exclusive advertising rights to the Taylor and Benson brand. She returned the document to its leather-bound embossed dossier and set it on the mahogany writing desk. Then she moved to the kitchen, where she quickly swallowed just one more delectable moule before sitting back on the living room couch, languidly waiting for Max to arrive.

As the cab sped through the darkening streets, Max Benson felt his heart racing. He kept checking his watch. He would have much preferred a lunch meeting at some place downtown. He stared out the window and thought of the woman he was about to meet: Edith Barrington. What a name. What a woman. The few times he had encountered her at her agency, she had never seemed quite real. She was one of those 'look at, but don't touch' types, a goddess with a class of breeding that Max could never hope to attain. As successful as he was in business, all his insecurities crept back when faced with a woman of this stature. Max wiped his brow. He had a sinking feeling that this evening was not going to go well for him.

After getting out of the taxi, Max entered the well-appointed lobby and announced himself to the attendant, who in turn telephoned Miss Barrington's apartment to inform her of his arrival. Taking the high-speed elevator, Max soon found himself on the 48th floor, tapping the gold ring that hung from the lion's mouth door-knocker of the suite.

As Max was wiping his brow one last time, the large oak door swung open and there Edith stood, exactly as he had imagined her. She was untouchable and perfect. Max felt his face turn scarlet as Edith extended her long bare arm and took his hand in hers. She was about to speak, while ushering him into her apartment, when suddenly she stopped and paled.

Later on, when Max would recount that moment to everyone he knew, he would tell them how Edith's eyelids fluttered ever so gently just before releasing the loudest and most explosive fart he had ever heard.

Lepidoptera

Who would have thought that Elmer Watkins would go out and get himself killed? But there it was, on the front page of the morning paper. It was only four or five lines, but you couldn't miss it, not unless you were totally absorbed in Elizabeth Taylor and Richard Burton's recent wedding in our fair city, or the two of them legally humping each other for the first time in one of our downtown hotel rooms:

'March 16th, 1964

*MONTREAL YOUTH KILLED IN MEXICO—Elmer Watkins, twenty-one, died as a result of a bus accident on a highway in Michoacán, Mex. More information will be available pending an investigation by the Mexican police. The parents of the deceased have flown to that country and will return with the body. Funeral arrangements to be announced at a later date.'

I had met Elmer about a year and a half prior, while making my first feeble attempt at university. I must admit that I didn't exactly take to him on the spot. In fact, when I first watched Elmer lug his huge frame through the hallways of the various faculty buildings, I was put right off. I mean, the guy was huge. I know it's wrong to go around disliking people just because of their appearance, and I'll admit I've always been kind of ashamed of the way I make snap judgments on sight. I guess that's why, when I later discovered that Elmer and I shared the same curriculum, I decided to be a little friendly. After all, what harm could it do, right? I approached him in the hallway outside the lecture hall after almost falling asleep during an incredibly boring lecture on semantics.

"Hi," I said. "I'm Barry Parsons. We seem to have been following each other around this past week."

Elmer's huge eyes bugged out in surprise. He looked sweaty and hot, and folds of flesh bulged out of a too-tight collar and closely knotted tie. It was an unseasonably hot September morning, and the prickly Harris Tweed jacket he was wearing didn't seem to be adding to his comfort. Being somewhat of a casual dresser, I was wearing my usual jeans and sandals. I looked down at my bare toes and began to wish that I hadn't initiated the conversation, but Elmer was right in there extending a damp plump hand and introducing himself.

Pressing on with my good Samaritan feeling, and knowing that our next lecture was not until two o'clock in the afternoon, I invited him to have lunch with me at a little place where I hung out on Stanley Street. He declined, saying that he was expected at home, but suggested that maybe he could join me the next day. I'll admit I was sort of relieved as I watched him lumber off down the hall. At least I had made the effort.

The following noon, Elmer was waiting for me. I had fallen asleep in philosophy class. The lecture room had become uncomfortably warm, and were it not for a kindly nudge on my elbow by Louise Franklin, who was sitting next to me, I would have certainly dozed right on through. I was gathering my books when Elmer was suddenly beside me, all tweedy and hot.

"Lunch," he said, raising a heavy arm and shoving a brown paper bag in my face.

"Huh?" I said.

"Our lunch date," Elmer said, smiling.

"Oh, yeah," I said. "I forgot about that. Well, I don't think they'd appreciate it if I ordered lunch and you sat there eating out of that paper bag. Why don't we make it some other time?"

The disappointment that flashed across his face was obvious. "But it's for both of us," he said, looking at me as though I should have known. "I thought we could get some soft drinks and eat on the grass near the library."

"That's real nice of you Elmer—I mean...that's kind of a nice idea." I put my arm on his shoulder and walked along the hall with him. "I'll get the drinks," I said, "and I'll meet you by the library steps in five minutes."

When I arrived at the library, Elmer was already sitting in a shady spot on the lawn. As I walked over to him, I couldn't help thinking he looked like a giant slug sprawled out on the grass. The brown paper bag had been opened, and an array of wax-papered sandwiches had been spread out around him.

"I told my mother all about you, and she made these for us," he said. "Trimmed or untrimmed?"

"What?" I asked.

"Crusts or no crusts? Some people don't like crusts on their sandwiches so Mother made both. There's egg, cheese and ham, and meatloaf and tomato. She says she'd like to meet you."

"I'll have the egg," I said, wondering what in the hell Elmer could have told his mother about me.

"No, they come together. The egg, cheese, and ham is one sandwich, and the meatloaf and tomato is the other. There are three each."

"The meatloaf and tomato will be fine," I said.

"Crusts or no crusts?"

"Dammit, Elmer, it doesn't make any difference," I answered. As I watched him perspire in his heavy wool jacket, I suddenly wished I were somewhere else.

"My mother said," Elmer began, his mouth overly full, "my mother said that a person is really lucky to make a good friend."

"Look, Elmer," I said. "I mean...like, we only just met yesterday, and I don't think..." I stopped myself. "What I mean is, I could tell right off the bat that you're a good guy and everything, and I really would like to be your friend."

"I thought so," Elmer said, smiling. "What other reason would you have to come up to me after class? I don't get many people speaking to me."

"Well, to tell you the truth, Elmer, I don't see why. I mean you seem like a really nice guy."

Elmer's face suddenly went dark. "Kids used to make fun of me because I was fat," he said. "It's always been that way ever since I can remember."

"Yeah, but that was then, Elmer. Today people go for what's in your head, not what you look like." I was really laying it on thick. "Keep up with the times, dude—this is the 1960s! Things are different now."

"Not much different for me," Elmer said, starting on his third sandwich. "Things are always pretty much the same for me."

I looked at him. "They don't have to be, you know."

"How so?" Elmer asked.

"Well, for starters, Elmer, it's bloody hot out. Why don't you take off your jacket?"

"I sort of feel more comfortable with it on," he said, shading his eyes as the sun passed over a gap in the protective tree.

"Yeah, well I think I'd better get going now, Elmer. It was a real nice sandwich. Thank your mother for me."

"But we don't have our next class until two o'clock," Elmer said, digging into the brown bag, "and you've only been here about ten minutes."

"I know," I said, "but I'm cutting classes this after-noon. I have to get together with some friends."

Elmer frowned. "You shouldn't cut classes," he said disapprovingly, and then added, "She wanted

155

to know if you would like to come for supper tomorrow night. My mother, she wanted to know."

"Your mother? Oh, I don't think I can, Elmer, but thank her for me anyway. Maybe some other time—"

"She said that Friday night would be alright too, if you couldn't make it tomorrow."

"I'm getting a lift up to the cottage with some friends. Probably leave early Friday evening," I said.

"Oh, I see." Elmer looked at me dejectedly. "Are you sure that you won't change your mind about cutting classes?"

"Fuck, Watkins," I exploded. "It's not really any of your goddamn business, is it?"

He looked like I had just slapped him in the face.

I stared down at the empty wax paper wrappers on the grass. I felt like a jerk. I mean, the poor guy didn't seem to have a friend in the world. "What the hell, Elmer," I said. "Tell your mother Friday night will be fine. I can always borrow my brother's car and drive to the cottage Saturday morning. I'll see you at class tomorrow."

I turned away and left him sitting there, sweating profusely.

Elmer's mother welcomed me at the door when I arrived, and I really had to look twice. She was so tiny and fragile that I couldn't believe that this woman had birthed Elmer. She told me that her son was upstairs taking a bath and would be downstairs shortly, and asked if I would care to join Elmer's father in the living room.

As I followed her, I became aware of the pungent smell of flowers. At first, I thought it was Mrs. Watkins' perfume, but then I noticed them— big orange blooms everywhere, sprouting out of pots, vases, and stands all over the house. They were all the same kind of flower, and all the same color. I don't know why, but just looking at them gave me the creeps.

Through the hall archway, I could see Mr. Watkins sitting on a sofa, reading a newspaper. I suddenly felt terribly uncomfortable in my old shirt and jeans. Or maybe it was my sandals. He stared at my feet when his wife ushered me into the living room and introduced me as Elmer's friend.

There was certainly no mistaking him for anyone else—he was every bit as fat as Elmer, maybe even more so. His neck bulged up from under his collar and, like his son, he wore a jacket and tie. He looked up from his newspaper when I sat down across from him, and made some kind of guttural sound. Fortunately, at that precise moment Elmer appeared and, not surprisingly, he was all buttoned up too.

He gave me such a somber "Hello," that I wondered what in the hell I was doing there. Without saying a word, Mr. Watkins stood up and I followed the both of them into the dining room.

Sitting at the Watkins' dining table was an extremely joyless event. The heat that had built up during the week seemed to have compacted itself into that one particular room. I wondered why no one turned on a fan; it was like sitting inside a cocoon. Mr. Watkins said nothing, but would occasionally emit these funny little sounds that only Mrs. Watkins seemed to understand. The meal was nauseatingly rich, and there seemed to be cream sauces over everything. I managed to get through most of it by concentrating on the wallpaper that ran the length of the room in horizontal floral stripes. I kept wishing that they ran from floor to ceiling, and thought of this each time Mrs. Watkins got up and went to the kitchen to bring out more food.

Without going into the details of the menu, one could easily account for the size of the men sitting on either side of me. Mr. Watkins would burp at the end of each course, and as if in response to a signal, his wife would pick up our plates and depart through the swinging door.

After making a few feeble attempts at light conversation, to which only Mrs. Watkins responded, and only with little nods, I divided my time between the wallpaper and watching everyone shovel food into their mouths.

When the meal finally came to an end, marked by a dessert of peaches, ice cream, and topping, Mrs. Watkins went back to the kitchen and returned with a huge chocolate cake covered with whipped cream and nuts. At this point, I really thought I was going to puke. As the feeling of nausea crept up inside me, I managed to get away with a large belch rather than the more spectacular emission. I stood up and excused myself, saying that I was feeling a bit dizzy from the heat and that I really thought I should be going.

"It's cooler up in my room," Elmer said, helping himself to a large piece of cake.

"Yes, why don't you boys take your cake upstairs?" Mrs. Watkins suggested. "It certainly is cooler up there, and Elmer can show you his collection."

Before I could express my desire to leave again, Elmer was up from his chair and out of the dining room. I had no choice but to follow him. Mr. Watkins stared at my feet again as I walked by him.

Butterflies.

The walls of Elmer's room were covered with glass-framed butterflies, wings stretched wide and pinned flat. There was even some kind of table with a glass arrangement over it. More butterflies. I have a particular hate-on for things like that, and always have. Now I could out-and-out hate Elmer too. The bed creaked noisily as he let his bulk settle down onto it. There was a chair at the far side of the bed, and he motioned for me to sit down.

"I think I'd better be off," I said. "I still may have a chance to get a lift up to the cottage. Thanks for supper."

"There's something that I want to discuss with you," Elmer said, picking at the nuts on the top of his chocolate cake.

"Look, Elmer," I said, "let me put it this way. I'm not in the least bit interested in hearing about your collection. I think killing live things and then putting them up for display is sick."

"I followed you," he said.

"Yeah, well," I replied, starting for the doorway. "But I've really got to be going now. See you around."

"You don't understand," Elmer said. "On Wednesday—when you said you were cutting classes in the afternoon to be with friends. I know where you went, and I know what goes on there."

I stared at him in disbelief. Imagine someone actually following me. I didn't know whether to be flattered or annoyed. In view of the fact that I anticipated what was coming next, I decided to be annoyed.

"There are naked women there and...and people use drugs," he continued. "I know all about it. You can get yourself into a lot of trouble there, Barry, and besides...it's not good for you. Being my friend, I feel it is for your own good that I—"

"Look, fat boy," I blurted out. "Why don't you mind your goddamned business and just stick to killing your fuckin' bugs!"

I was out of his room in a flash. No sooner was I on the street then I started feeling bad. But I couldn't figure out the hell why. I mean, he was the one who was spying. I didn't need a snoop in my life. And besides, what the fuck—I wasn't doing anything that wrong anyway.

I avoided Elmer the following Monday. I had just come back from a great weekend in the Laurentians, and when I arrived for my first lecture of the day I made a point of staying clear of him. I was standing next to Louise Franklin when I saw him heading my way, and I deliberately turned my back to him, interrupting a conversation that Louise was having with someone else. Then I chose the most occupied area of the lecture hall to sit in, so that when the two hours had passed, I could walk out of the room surrounded by other students.

I had an hour and a half between lectures, so I went down to the "Cage" on Stanley Street. Just before two o'clock I was on my way back to campus when I spotted him from a distance. He was trying to catch my attention, and had started to run in my direction. I was well on my way down the street when I started feeling stupid. I sat down on a bus stop bench and waited. He was out of breath, red-faced and wet. The top button of his collar was undone and his tie had been loosened. He couldn't talk, and just stood in front of me panting heavily. I moved over on the bench and made room for him. He sat down, and it seemed a full five minutes before he could breathe more easily.

"I'm sorry," he managed to get out. That, and nothing more.

"Okay," I said quietly.

"Did you have a good time up north?" he asked.

"Yeah, I had a blast."

"I've never been there," he said. "I've always stayed in the city. Even during the summer. Do your parents have a place up there?"

"No," I answered. "I rent the place with two other guys."

"Oh," he said, removing his jacket and folding it over his knees. I detected a distinct sound of disappointment in his voice. After a moment of silence, he turned to me. "I was just thinking," he said, "that if it belonged to your parents, maybe I could come up one time. But I guess if you rent it with other guys, they wouldn't want me there."

"Well, actually," I said, "they're not up there every weekend."

"Really?"

"Yeah, next weekend I'll be there on my own."

"Oh?"

I looked at him. "Ya wanna come?"

I don't think I ever saw a face light up with so much gratitude in my life.

"That would be wonderful!" Elmer blurted out.

"I'll pick you up Saturday morning," I said, standing. "But remember—don't bug me too much when we're up there, okay?

The following Saturday morning I drove to Elmer's house. I had borrowed my brother's car, and stocked it with the supplies we would need for the weekend. Elmer was already out on the front porch waiting for me. He was wearing a white polo shirt tucked inside a new pair of jeans. His waistline must have measured a good forty-six inches, and the heavy denim stood out like cardboard around each leg. He was sitting on an old suitcase, the real heavy kind with the squared off edges.

"Hey, man," I hollered through the open car window. "We're only going for two days, you know."

He came down the steps and opened the back door of the car, putting the suitcase on the floor. I opened the front door for him and he got in beside me.

"I have some things that I wanted to bring along," he said.

"None of those bugs you collect, I hope"

"No, nothing like that," he said, smiling.

As luck would have it, no sooner had we turned off the Laurentian auto-route than the sky turned a shitty black, and down it came. It wasn't just a quick shower, but a deluge that made it difficult for me to see the road. We finally made it to the cottage and parked the car. In the few seconds it took us to unpack and reach the front door, we were both thoroughly soaked.

"We'd better get into something dry," I suggested. "I'll light the oil lamps and get a fire going. Better give me your wet things."

Elmer set his suitcase down on the floor. "I haven't got anything else to wear, just these jeans and the shirt that I've got on."

"Well, you'd better get out of them and put a blanket around you. Here," I said, tossing him a towel and taking a wool blanket out of the closet. "What the hell is in that suitcase anyway?"

I took his jeans and shirt from him and put them over a chair near the fireplace. "With any luck, these should be dry in a few hours."

I got out of my own wet things and dried myself off. I put on a fresh pair of jeans and placed my wet things beside Elmer's. "Come one, man, give me your underwear and socks too. You can't keep those on."

Shielding his naked body with the blanket, Elmer reluctantly took off his underwear.

"I suppose these are the only ones you've brought, too," I said, taking them from him. "So, what the fuck's in that suitcase?"

He reached down, holding the blanket tightly around him and unfastened the funny-looking clip locks. The top of the case released, and he opened it. "This," he said.

"What?" I asked, looking into the suitcase and seeing nothing but a paper bag and a pile of note books.

"These...these things that I've written. I wanted you to see them. I've never shown them to anyone before."

I reached down to touch a pile of note books.

"No," Elmer stopped me. "Start with these first."

He pointed to a second pile that looked yellowed and frayed. "I arranged them in proper order last night."

I picked up the first book and opened it. It was written in childish script and was signed Elmer Watkins, nine years old.

Today was my birthday. I had a party and it was fun. Mummy and Daddy were there and we had good things to eat. I got presents too.

"Elmer," I said, looking up at him. "Do you really want me to read this stuff?"

He said nothing and just nodded.

Today I picked up a pretty marigold that was growing at the side of the school entrance, and Michael Felton threw a stick at me. He said he threw it because I am fat. Tonight, Mummy made my favorite dessert. Cherry pie, topped with whipped cream and colored candy bits.

"Elmer," I said, "I don't think I can read all this stuff. There's so much, and besides—"

"But I want you to read it."

I saw the hurt in his eyes. *Aw, shit*, I thought, and continued reading.

He had detailed everything; from the special chocolate fudge cake his mother had labored over on the occasion of his eleventh birthday to his first wank. His high school days were filled with dozens of unkind remarks and relentless bullying, all connected to his 'morbid obesity,' a term that the school nurse had referred to when doing a weigh-in as part of the physical health program.

Each notebook contained pages devoted to his love for flowers, and a growing obsession with butterflies. He described how he would gently catch them with the net he had purchased at a pet shop; the first killing jar he had fashioned; the poisoned saturated cotton balls that would ultimately kill the butterfly once it had been caught and sealed in the jar; the removal of the dead insect from the jar; and finally, the pinning of it through the thorax as it dried out on wax paper. It was really starting to turn my stomach. "Elmer," I said. "I can't read any more of this"

He looked at me and said nothing.

I felt uncomfortable. I listened to the sound of the rain make a steady beat on the cottage roof. "Not much of a start to your weekend, is it?" I said, putting down the note book and looking away.

"It doesn't matter," Elmer said. "I'm enjoying myself just being here."

"Yeah, well that's good," I said. "You know, Elmer...I think that one of your basic problems is that you spend too much time alone...y'know what I mean? You have to get out more. Really make an effort to meet people."

"It's not easy," he said, "when you look like a—"

"Cut that out!" I interrupted. "Have you ever thought of trying to do something about it? I mean, haven't you ever heard of the word exercise?"

"Of course," he said, "but I'm not very good at it. They always laughed at me in school. You read about it yourself."

"Elmer," I said, brainstorming another one of my good Samaritan ideas that I was sure to regret later. "You and I are gonna work out at the gym, before classes. We'll do it two or three days a week.

The place is empty early in the morning, and I know enough about simple exercise. We may not make a he-man out of you, but we'll sure as hell get you into better shape. Here," I said, tossing him an apple. "Munch on this while I get some steaks going."

"I brought some chocolate bars too," he said.

"Where are they?" I asked.

"In the paper bag in the suitcase," he said, reaching down for it.

"Give that to me," I said.

I took the bag from him and looked inside. There must have been about forty dollars' worth of chocolate. I reached into the bag, took out one bar and handed it to him, and brought the paper sack into the kitchen with me.

"You gotta cut out that sweet stuff, Elmer," I hollered back, "And don't go fucking up once you get home. Otherwise, no go at the gym. You guys attack food like army ants at your house."

Elmer was silent.

"Hey!" I said, sticking my head out the door. "Move your ass and check the clothes to see if they're dry. Then come in the kitchen and help me out. I ain't your mother, y'know."

Meeting Elmer at the gym at eight o'clock the following Tuesday morning meant having to get up an hour earlier than usual. I was kind of hoping that he wouldn't show up, and then I could use that as an excuse for not following through. Even though I had extended the offer with all sincerity, I felt cheated out of sixty minutes of snooze time.

But, sure enough, Elmer was there waiting for me. He had brought along a canvas bag, and he unzipped it proudly, showing me a new pair of gym trunks and tennis shoes. We went into the locker room and changed our clothes. I decided to start with simple laps around the room. Three times, fairly slowly. Elmer was out of breath after the first lap, and by the third I knew I was pushing him.

"Easy man, easy, "I said. "Let's stop now and rest a bit." After he had caught his breath, I started him on the exercises that I could best remember from my days at high school.

"C'mon Elmer," I said. "Watch," I demonstrated. "Arms forward raise, upward stretch, rise on the toes, inhale. Sideward lower, slowly press the arms back, and exhale." I did this twice, and he followed my example.

"No bad, not bad," I said, praising him. "Now, stand with your arms at your side. Then sideward raise, upward stretch, inhale, forward bend, and rise. Arms sideward, lower, exhale."

This was more difficult, and he looked at me with a pained expression after attempting it.

"Never mind," I said. "If you think that one was hard, this one's gonna knock the shit out of you, but you gotta remember...it takes a lot of time and effort if you wanna get in shape."

I went over to a row of bars that ran horizontally against the wall from ceiling to floor. I lay back, catching the instep of my shoes under the lowest bar. With hands clasped behind my head, I raised it, extending my spine, and pressed my elbows forward. I repeated it six times.

"That one's not for today," I said. "Let's go through those first ones again and then call it. We shouldn't do too much at first anyway, but you've got the general idea for starters. We'll go through this same routine three times a week. You'll probably feel a bit sore tomorrow, but that's the price you have to pay. Now, lets' get this over and then hit the showers."

Elmer waited in the locker room, fully clothed, until I had finished showering.

"Hey, boy!" I said, slapping him playfully with my towel. "Where were you? There's nothing to be shy about. I've seen one before." Elmer looked away, embarrassed.

"So...what's for your lunch?" I asked.

"Two egg sandwiches and a Hershey."

"Sounds good," I said, drying myself off and getting into my clothes. I shoved my sweat shirt and trunks into my gym bag. "I'll see you at class. Don't drown in the shower."

The three months that followed brought incredible changes in Elmer's appearance. He worked out at the gym every day. I had stopped going after a couple of weeks, but he was following through with the arduous task that I had set for him. As if that were not enough, he had even bought himself exercise equipment to work out with at home. By the end of December, he must have dropped about forty pounds.

In mid-January, I had several course changes that kept me in the buildings on the other side of campus. That, plus the fact that Brenda from Toronto had entered my life during the Christmas holidays, prevented me from having any contact with Elmer until late spring. Brenda was visiting me and we were strolling on the campus grounds one Saturday morning when I walked right by him. He had said hello; at least Brenda had heard him.

"Who was that?" she asked, her eyes big and wide. I turned around, and he was standing there, smiling.

"Elmer?" I questioned.

A lean but well-built young man in blue jeans, deeply tanned, flashed white teeth in our direction. His facial features were finely chiseled, with bone structure that had obviously been there all along. He extended his hand to me, and I reluctantly introduced him to Brenda.

"What have you been up to, Elmer?" I asked. "Been hibernating or something? Where'd you get that tan?"

"Flew down to Tampa for Easter vacation. Got to keep moving while you can," he answered, smiling at Brenda.

"Elmer, you look fantastic," I said. "I just can't get over it. Are you still collecting butterflies?" I threw that in to help Brenda close her gaping mouth.

"Not much time for that anymore," he said, "Look, we'll have to get together soon. So much has happened. I've got a class in three minutes. Tried to quit the Saturday morning lectures, but just couldn't manage it. I'll call you. Really nice meeting you, Brenda."

"Well, I'll be a son-of-a-bitch," I said under my breath as he disappeared from view.

"What?" Brenda asked.

"Nothing," I answered. "It's not important."

I miraculously managed to get through my final exams in spite of the distraction of having Brenda in my life. Commuting weekends was making me a nervous wreck, even though she did her share of traveling as well. I convinced her to persuade her parents to let her continue her education in Montreal in the fall, and they agreed. I found myself more relaxed and studying much harder during the new term. It was great to have Brenda with me. I was in love, and I knew I had a good thing.

It didn't even occur to me that I had not seen Elmer around campus when the new semester started, and then in March, I read about him in the newspaper.

I watched for the funeral announcement, and took Brenda into the chapel with me. The room that we were directed to was filled with flowers. I was surprised only Mr. and Mrs. Watkins were there, sitting together facing the open casket. I don't think they remembered me, for they stared back with blank eyes when I approached them.

I walked over to the coffin and looked down. Elmer's face was gaunt, and his skin, which had been richly tanned by the Mexican sun, was stretched tightly against his cheek-bones. They had given him some kind of powder job which seemed to have aged him considerably. Mr. Watkins joined me at the coffin, and Brenda took her place beside the frail little woman, sitting down beside her and taking hold of her hand. Mr. Watkins' collar was still too tight, and his neck bulged out. He looked into the mahogany casket, holding onto the edge.

"It was a freak accident," he said. "A tire blew out on the bus and it hit a street lamp. The pole crashed through the bus window, piercing my son's chest, impaling him to his seat. Other passengers were injured, but Elmer was the only one killed."

There was a moment of awkward silence as Mr. Watkins stared at the displays of marigolds surrounding the casket. "Elmer loved these flowers, you know," he said.

"Yeah, and butterflies too," I said, motioning to Brenda that it was time to go. "He let me read about it once."

———•———

The transformation which takes place in the lifecycle of a butterfly is great and precipitous. The egg is laid either singly or in groups. After a period of weeks, a caterpillar appears and embarks on its life's mission, which is to feed voraciously, grow and molt. When it has amassed enough food reserve in its lardaceous body, it cloaks itself within a hard covering called a pupa. Changes signaling an astonishing metamorphosis can be observed, until finally a butterfly breaks forth to unfold its wings and ascend majestically.

The duration of the life history varies, determined by the species.

Elmer W.

Jalna's
Delight

Delight

When she saw the rolls of pink '1/2 price' stickers left unattended on a shelf next to the pomegranates, Jalna grabbed three rolls and quickly put them in her purse. There were at least five hundred 'reduced for quick sale' stickers in each roll.

From that time on, shopping at the upscale Food Emporium was sheer delight, for everything Jalna bought was always marked half-price.

The Simple
Truth

Merle lay there, picking at the coverlet of the huge hospital bed. It had been another uncomfortable night, and the painkillers they had given her had worn off long ago. She was going to buzz for the nurse and ask for more, but decided against it. Today was visiting day, and she didn't want to be too drowsy.

The sun was starting to streak through the side of the window shades. The small jeweled clock on the night table read six forty-five. It wouldn't be long now.

Merle rang for the nurse. She knew that the fat-faced one from the night before was still on duty.

"And how are we today, Mrs. Pottman?" the nurse asked when she finally arrived.

"And how should I be today, with you coming in ten minutes after I rang for you?"

"Now, Mrs. Pottman, I was right outside your door. You know it wasn't ten minutes. Here, let me make you more comfortable."

The nurse fluffed up the pillows behind Merle's back. Merle winced.

"Pain bad today, Mrs. Pottman? I'll bring you something for it as soon as we brighten up your room a bit. It's a lovely day outside." The nurse walked over to one of the windows and began lifting the shade.

"Leave it as it is," Merle said.

"But Mrs. Pottman, surely you don't want to stay here in the dark, do you?"

"Leave the shades as they are. Would you please bring me some coffee?"

"Certainly, Mrs. Pottman." The nurse hurried out the door. She returned moments later with a Styrofoam cup.

"Not that stuff you've been drinking all night," Merle snapped. "I'd like some fresh coffee, if you don't mind, and in a proper cup and saucer."

"Then you'll have to wait a bit until breakfast," the nurse said, setting the coffee down by the table next to Merle's bed. "I'm afraid I can't leave the floor. Here, take one of these." The nurse produced a bottle of pills from her pocket.

"I don't want one of those."

"But you'll feel much better." She placed a pill down beside the coffee.

"Today is visiting day, and I don't want to be all doped up."

"Well, how about taking only a half?"

"No. If you can't bring me a fresh cup of coffee, then get out. That's what I rang you for."

"Mrs. Pottman—"

"Get out," Merle said, a little louder than she had intended.

The nurse gave her a look of dismay and left the room. Merle waited for her to close the door before she swallowed the pill and took a quick gulp of the coffee.

How she hated this place!

She slowly lifted herself out of the bed and made her way into the bathroom. There she brushed her teeth and washed her face. Going back into the room, she selected a fresh dress from the closet and picked out one of the newly coiffed wigs that she had recently ordered. She sat down at the dressing table and carefully placed the hair piece over the remaining wisps of hair still on her head. She checked her appearance in the mirror.

She looked awful.

She stood up, lifted the shades covering the window, and let the warm summer sun come streaming into the room and onto her face. The flowers next to the well-manicured lawn looked beautiful in the early morning light.

Merle sighed. The pill had started to take effect and the pain was beginning to ease. The orderly would soon be in with breakfast. She settled back in an arm chair in the corner of the room and waited.

Merle had always prided herself on her looks and her good taste. Her late husband, Eddie Pottman,

had taught her how to dress and how to appreciate the finer things in life. He worked for The
Mercantile Bank, and during their thirty-year
marriage they had travelled to exotic places all
throughout the year. It would be a different kind of
life, Eddie had warned her before their marriage,
not the kind she and her high-school girlfriends
had envisioned for themselves. But while the like-
lihood of not having children was bothersome to
Merle, having a palatial home in Connecticut and
the opportunity to see far-away worlds outside of
her own was a choice she never regretted. When
Eddie died of a heart attack ten years ago, she
was devastated.

After breakfast, Ruth was the first to arrive. She
explained that she could only stay for a short visit
because she had left Sol at home with the grand-
kids, and they usually drove him crazy after only a
half an hour.

She told Merle how marvelous she looked, how
much they missed her at the club this summer,
and that she was sure to be back in no time and
probably beat them all in the bridge tournament
in the fall. Merle hated her for that. She knew

that Ruth came early only because she wanted to leave early and get out to the club. When the door opened and the others began to arrive, Ruth suddenly stood up. "No sense in letting the room get too crowded," she said, kissing Merle on the cheek and scurrying out the door. *What a phony*, Merle thought.

After Ruth had gone, Gertie came up to her chair. She was the poor one in the family. Her husband drove a cab, and no one let her forget it. On several occasions, Merle had to make up the rent money that Gertie couldn't pay on their tiny bungalow. She brought Merle some drooping flowers that she had picked from her backyard garden.

Merle's niece, Rebecca, came next, bringing her two overweight children, Marvin and Beverly. Better that, she thought, than that idiot husband of hers, who thought that every word that came out of Merle's mouth was deserving of his irritating, donkey-bray laugh. How she loathed that man. When Rebecca told Marvin to give his Aunty Merle a kiss, Marvin said no. Little Beverly did what she was told while Marvin got a swat on the ear.

A twinge of pain shot through Merle's body at about twelve o'clock, and Jacob, her younger brother, noticed.

"Merle, maybe we should leave you and you should get some rest?" he said.

"It's nothing, Jake. Just a spasm. They come and go."

He can't wait to get back to Sophie, she thought. Her sister-in-law had never once come to visit her at the hospital. Not even once. Just phone calls. Jacob explained that Sophie was confined to bed with another cold, but after next week maybe everything would be alright and she could come to see her. *Yeah right*, Merle thought.

The orderly came in with lunch, and the others, who now numbered more than five, began to file out of the room. Merle knew they had been eagerly waiting for this moment to finally make their exit.

She took a quick smell of the food and pushed it away. Why did these people come to see her? Just to patronize her? She wanted to be alone. Why couldn't they understand that?

Suddenly Dodie Greenberg, a neighbor from down the street and just back from Miami, barged in. "Too hot for this time of year, even at bargain rates," she said, giving Merle a kiss on the forehead and plunking her seashell-embroidered straw bag down by the side of Merle's chair. "A little something for you," Dodie said.

Merle looked down at a small plastic soap dish with a papered bar of scented soap, along with a small jar of hand cream. *Freebies from the hotel bathroom,* she thought. *What a cheapskate!*

Her pain came back again, this time sharp as a knife. She rang for the nurse and asked Dodie if she wouldn't mind joining the others in the hall. Merle stumbled back to her bed and waited for the nurse to come. Outside she could hear them whispering in the hall, whispering about her. Why were they still there? They were hypocrites, every one of them. In better days, when she had had her health, she had outshone them all. Now they were all watching her. Watching her lose her grip. She resented their pity.

She had never liked any of them, anyway.

Suddenly the stabs of pain became unbearable. Merle leaned over and rang for the nurse again. Where was she? *Where was that nurse?*

On a wet morning seven months later, the stone was unveiled, and they were all there to watch it. It was a particularly beautiful piece. Not too ornate, and in good taste. "The way Merle would have wanted it," Ruth said, and Dodie Greenberg agreed. They numbered about seventy-five in all, and after the rabbi finished the chant, they all moved closer to the stone. Gertie leaned forward and placed a single flower at its base. Rebecca smiled at the stone and said, "Aunt Merle always did love the finer things in life."

The chiseled marking read:

'Loved by family and friends
Not to be forgotten, and always in our hearts'

And that, after all, was the simple truth.

A Good Cleaning Is a Good Cleaning

Daisy Bilbar smiled with satisfaction as her printer spat out several more sheets of wallet-sized business cards:

HOUSE CLEANING TO PERFECTION!
First day, free of charge. No obligation after that
Ongoing reasonable rates
Call for references. (Tel # on back of card)

There were about twenty senior-inhabited residential buildings that Daisy had already scurried in and out of that week, leaving these business cards thumb-tacked to bulletin boards and placed in ornate bowls on elegant lobby credenzas.

The elders who called her, most of them octogenarians, were only too happy to have a cleaning of their apartments. Even if they never used Miss Bilbar's services again, a good cleaning is a good cleaning. Furthermore, Daisy's references were impeccable; and even more, the first day would be free. What a *deal*!!

They had all thanked Daisy after her day's work. She knew that she would never hear from any of them again.

Now, spread out on Daisy's kitchen table in colorful array, were dozens of opioids, stimulants, sedatives, and tranquilizers all taken from bathroom medicine cabinets; just a few pills culled carefully from each bottle, not enough to make a discernible difference in the failing eyesight of her unassuming clients.

Sold at street value, they would fetch a tidy sum.

Daisy smiled again and reminded herself to thank her two sisters, who, with their polished voices in contrived plumy English accents, had provided the very best of telephone references.

Muriel
And The
Good Eats

The middle years had not been kind to Muriel Tweedsmuire. Her job at The Daily Factor as food critic had left her with an insatiable craving for exotic fare, and when the tabloid folded, so did Muriel. Days of dining and critiquing for the morning paper had come to an abrupt end.

Not one to make friends easily, and known to be very sharp of tongue, she had no contacts to fall back on in her search for new employment. Since she was no longer able to make a living as adjudicator of gastronomic delights, and being too overbearing for the foodie shows on the tele (although word had it that she had auditioned several times), the repugnant articulé (as the French would say) she showed when angered was a definite impediment. Thus Muriel resigned herself to living off the sale of her extraordinary and exquisite Biedermeier table linens, which had enjoyed impeccable and loving care in her family for generations.

Within a very short time, however, all of these handsome heirlooms had been sold.

Not being a "meat and two veg" gal, and finding it impossible to change her diet away from the finer delicacies of life's palate, Muriel soon discovered that all of her monies had completely run out. Going on 'the dole' became a necessity, and she moved into a council flat in the SW9. It was an insufferable humiliation, more so because she could not free herself from the scintillating aromatic memories that at one time welcomed her daily arrival at the finest eateries in London town. Just thinking of a fabulous grand mushroom feuillete, plated with a finely seasoned steak tartar, would render Muriel faint of heart.

Attired in her Sunday best (a buttoned-down black-grey dress with jacket and veiled pillbox hat), Muriel would escape her flat and spend a noon hour at Jarrod's. It was one of her favorite upscale food markets, and her most cherished once-a-week venture. Wednesday was "Taste and Sample Day," during which Muriel would help herself to a large plateful of fougasse (leaf-shaped bread with parsley and sea salt). "Just browsing dear, thanks ever so," she would say, and under her breath an almost inaudible "and bugger off," to the clerk who had addressed her.

After one particularly delectable Wednesday at Jarrod's, Muriel decided that she just couldn't face returning home straight away. It was a balmy July afternoon, and the noisy doings of the uncouth brats running around her working-class neighborhood would be impossible to endure. She instead took the tube to Archway Station and then caught the bus that would take her to Waterdown Park. She knew that the country like surroundings there were beautiful at that time of year.

Muriel was strolling down Swain's Lane, adjacent to Highgate cemetery, and snacking upon some bits of the delicious Lithuanian marzipan that she had, with almost sleight of hand, spirited away into her Italian satchel while at Jarrod's, when she noticed a large motorcade slowly approaching the cemetery. It was most impressive; sleek black limousines, ten in all, trailed after a massive flower-topped hearse. Several elegant automobiles followed, and one by one, beautifully dressed men and women stepped out of the vehicles into the pathway. Muriel, appropriately dressed for the occasion in her Jarrod's "Taste and Sample" outfit, took it upon herself to follow the procession at a respectful distance.

By the time she reached the burial site at the top of the hill, Muriel was out of breath. She leaned on an ornamental gravestone for support. She had not expected the climb to be so hard on her legs. Just as the ceremony was ending, a smartly dressed gentleman suddenly approached her.

"Mi scusi singorina...mi sembra stanca. Se non ha un passaggio per il pasto funerale posso offrigglielo voleniteri."

Muriel could only make out two words: "funeral and pasta."

She gingerly touched her pillbox hat and, lowering the tulle veil, nodded in the affirmative.

Her muted but constant sobs, while holding a lacy handkerchief to her nose, dampened any attempts at conversation that may have been deemed appropriate during the automobile ride from the cemetery to the Mayfair district. Muriel couldn't speak Italian, didn't know the deceased, did not want to be involved in verbal exchange in any language, and more importantly, it was long past tea time and she was bloody hungry.

And there, in a great hall, awaiting Muriel, was a wondrous spread of magnificent food, presented in such a spectacular fashion that it took her breath away. There were trays of porchetta, thinly-sliced and slow-roasted; charcoal-grilled red peppers with a spicy Balsamic reduction; manzo rastao (a spicy roasted beef, stacked with cheddar, oven-baked onions and smeared with horseradish mayo) and pollo alla griglia (a flamed-grilled breast of chicken, topped with fire-blackened red peppers, provolone, and a delightful chipotle sauce), all displayed on at least ten tables of food. The dishes wafted miraculous aromas from their open tureens.

Muriel didn't speak to anyone, and luckily no one spoke to her. She left the hall completely sated, walked down the cobble-stoned laneway, and looked for the first convenient bus that would take her to the underground and back to the SW9.

The next morning, Muriel awoke with a start—a sudden idea flashed into her brain that seemed like 'manna from heaven,' as it were. The London Times, The Telegraph, The Guardian, and The Evening Standard all had important roles to play. And so began Muriel's daily trips to the newspaper kiosk, wire-framed buggy-wagon clanking noisily behind her. Not just these newspapers did she buy, but a dozen or so, each with their tidy obituary columns. And why bother with just cemetery rituals? If an address was printed for a reception, with the given time thereof, Muriel would skip the burial altogether. Saturdays' papers were the best, when notices for the following seven days would appear.

Week after week, her datebook would fill up in a menu-like fashion: Greek, Italian, Spanish, French...She would arrive a quarter of an hour early at the address indicated, and keep a short distance away from the reception doors or gates. Then she would position and pace her entrance carefully to coincide perfectly with an approaching group. Her black dress, pillbox hat, and lowered veil blended in beautifully with each newly-found entourage of mourners.

Muriel soon discovered that there were not only funeral receptions to partake of. Newspaper social columns offered many other sweet and savory enticements. At an eightieth birthday reception for Benekykt Kucharski, in the vestibule of The Lady of Czestochowa Catholic Polish Church, Muriel happily sampled nalesniki, bigos, and some flaki and plaki (served with spiced apple sauce). Mme Lefevere's fundraiser for the Orphans of Calais offered an equally succulent fare of pissaladiere (truly unforgettable) and beautifully shaped rillettes. And how could Muriel not attend the afternoon garden party held by Adelpha Diodorus (in honor of her own daughter's fifth born) on the lawns of the Greek Orthodox Church of St. Lazarus and St. Andrew in Forest Gate? There Muriel wore her champagne-colored pillbox and off-white gold-buttoned double-breasted suit, and spent the entire afternoon gorging on wonderful taramosalata and a superb tirokafteri. What a glorious summer of feasting!

It was in the middle of September, on a particularly dark and cloudy day, that Muriel experienced her downfall.

She had been anticipating a particular 'food event' for weeks, and had even tried to eat a little less the week before so that she could indulge herself more fully on this particular occasion. Muriel knew that once a year, around the start of autumn, no serious food lover in Turkey could be absent from the world-renowned International Gaziantep

Gastronomy Festival. And so, when the Turkish Embassy announced an exclusive indoor event to mark the festival in London, and included a list of invited dignitaries and esteemed guests, Muriel was determined to be celebrating among them.

Muriel boarded the Knightsbridge bus, and within a half-hour was devouring superlative Turkish sweets of the most incredible lightness of texture. She was reaching for another tulumba (cylinders of soft baked pastry soaked in a sugary syrup) when suddenly a small piece of that confection, which had somehow found its way to the polished floor of the embassy ballroom, caught Muriel's right shoe at a most unexpected moment. In the blink of an eye, she did a backward somersault in an arse-over-tit fashion and slid, feet first, under a table of firin sutlac (a baked milk-and-rice custard pudding with a crusty top speckled with brown spots, where the baking process has lightly singed it).

Muriel winced in pain as she was lifted off the wheeled stretcher that had carried her through the old corridors of the Royal London Hospital and hoisted onto a hospital bed.

Several hours later she was awakened from surgery by her council flat solicitor, Mr. Ramsbottom, who immediately began advising her. He told her that although she had been flagrantly trespassing at a state event, the Turkish Embassy had announced that there would be no lawsuit. Additionally, in a gesture of goodwill, they felt that a small sum should be offered; enough to cover what the National Health would not. Muriel's left leg, cumbersomely fitted with a cast that ran the length from hip to toe, was suspended a foot and a half in the air. In a fortnight, Mr. Ramsbottom told her, she would be fitted with a walking cast, and then released from hospital.

A forlorn and disheveled-looking nurse's assistant arrived with a breakfast of boiled oats, mashed banana and prune, all in one bowl.

Muriel glumly chewed on a squashed prune as she listened half-heartedly to the solicitor's drone: "My dear Miss Tweedsmuire, when we are involved in an act that is of either willful or active negligence, distinguished, that is, from a mere omission of duty, which causes injury or invasion to another person, especially, in the former, of their property, or if you would," he continued, "to enter illegally or improperly, without any prior given authority

213

or consent, upon the real property of another, or to invade, as it were—"

"Bollocks!" Muriel cursed loudly.

Mr. Ramsbottom blushed. "I'll have you know, Miss Tweedsmuire," he rushed on, "that the Turkish Embassy has informed me that they consider trespassing among Turkish dignitaries at their state event a *serious threat* to national security. Furthermore, they have stated that they *will*, if need be, *press charges* against you if, over the next year, you are found trespassing *anywhere* in the vicinity of Greater London. And if you are even remotely suspected of trespassing during that period, the Turkish Embassy has most firmly assured me that they will, and without any hesitation, report you immediately to the MI5 for *international espionage*!"

Muriel glared at the man. "My tea is getting cold, and I hate bloody prune," she snarled.

It was one month later, with walking cast removed, that Muriel ventured back out into the world of fashionable edibles. A little shop in Kensington had advertised a first-come-first-serve taste of a doulette d'avesnes (a very strong and spicy French cheese) paired with a six-ounce glass of a robust dark German beer. Muriel was first in line, having set her alarm an extra hour earlier that morning.

"Muriel? Muriel Tweedsmuire? "

"Oh, bloody hell!" cursed Muriel under her breath, as she heard her name being called out a third time from somewhere behind her in the curving queue to the shop doors. She lowered her sunglasses, and with a slight turn of her neck, looked back and recognized the caller. It was that detestable cow, Lucy Bellmore, the one who wrote that insipid "Home and Hearth" column at the now defunct Daily Factor.

Lucy maneuvered her way up to the front of the queue where Muriel was standing, collar up, neck receding turtle-like into her linen jacket.

"Why, Muriel, it *is* you! Where have you been? Do you know that half of The Food for Life Network has been looking for you?

"What on Earth are you talking about, woman?" Muriel said, lowering her dark glasses to the tip of her nose and peering over them.

"Why, the show...the *show* of course! You auditioned for the studio a year ago, don't you remember? Now there's a new show that's going into production—it's called *Hellion in the Kitchen*—and the producers want *you*! There are four of us... food adjudicators...and we judge meals prepared by young chefs. You would be the female counterpart of what's his name, on that other show—you know, the one with the terribly bad manners who always swears at everyone? Muriel, *where* have you been? We all thought you were *dead*!"

Muriel was tempted to shout out, "Quit your squawking, you dumb nut!" but something made her hold her tongue. Suddenly pleasant thoughts began to float into her brain...images of filet of sole, sautéed with almonds...mussels cooked in white wine and garlic purée...perhaps a grilled tiger shrimp or two. After all, if what Lucy had just told her were true, very soon she would be eating happily again...and for a very long time...

"Darling, Lucy," Muriel purred in the sweetest voice she could conjure. "How have you been, *dear heart*?

The Gates
to Heaven

to Heaven

She quickly put the frozen food packages into the freezer. Everything else was left on the counter for unpacking later.

Her three-year-old son was awaiting her in the car, and she could see him in the driveway through the kitchen window. He was happily playing with the toy steering wheel that his father had fastened to the dashboard of the car.

When she glanced out the window again, her heart stopped.

The car was moving.

Her son had released the car's handbrake, and the vehicle was moving slowly backwards down the drive towards the street. She cried out to him.

Frightened, the little boy grabbed at the car door handle, lifted himself out, and ran to the back of the moving car, and in doing so, opened the gates to heaven.

God's
Creatures

She was very old.

The lines that creased her sunken cheeks stretched parchment-like across the bones of her dry, sunburnt face. Her body lurched with each tentative probe of a wooden cane and, always holding on to the iron bar of a tattered buggy with her other hand, she moved forward in a lopsided manner.

She smelled bad

The old black sweater and skirt that never seemed to leave her body reeked from months of unwashed neglect. Her shoes, sandal-like in appearance, slid dangerously under her fragile frame as she hobbled from one sidewalk dustbin to another, hoping to find a discarded treasure to add to her collection.

I had watched her for years as she combed the alleyway trash cans of my neighborhood, mumbling to herself while shooing away something unseen that hovered around her face.

On that particular day, I had seen her make her way on to the middle of the road, mindless of the blaring horns of oncoming vehicles. There she retrieved a dead pigeon that had just fallen from the sky, while an angry falcon squawked overhead at the loss of its prey. Carefully she placed the bird on top of the worn buggy, and continued on.

I followed her, wondering what she was going to do with the dead bird. Would she take it home and cook it?

As she approached an inner-city park, I discreetly kept my distance.

With much effort, she stationed her buggy upright. Gently taking the pigeon in one hand, and supporting herself on the side arm of a park bench, she lowered her body to a kneeling position on the grassy path beneath her.

She lay the pigeon down and reached into the side pocket of her sweater, producing some kind of shiny metal object which was difficult for me to see.

After several minutes, I couldn't resist a closer view.

Her hands were covered with dirt. She had been using a silver soup spoon to dig a hole in the soft earth. She looked up at me.

"Every one of God's creatures deserves respect," she said, placing the bird in the hole.

"Amen to that," I said softly, and walked away, leaving the woman to her work.

The End

It began twenty minutes into the first act.

Marvin Shay, in his role as Sir Guy Fenwick, was about to receive the cue for his entrance. Lady Birchmount had just stormed off stage, leaving her daughter, Pamela, sobbing on the park bench.

"You're on," the prompter whispered.

Marvin took a deep breath.

This was the night he had waited for. The years of chorus and understudy work had finally paid off. Although his name was not on the Manhattan theatre marquis, it was listed third on the Playbill Program. He had dreamed of an opening night like this: a filled-to-capacity house with not a seat to be had, including in the 'gods,' assuring him that every important critic would be observing him that evening.

Marvin entered stage right, walking towards the bench and the crying girl. He took Pamela's hand in his and began to deliver the monologue which would hopefully bring the audience and critics alike to their feet with thunderous applause.

But after just four lines, Marvin froze.

The sound started almost imperceptibly at first, a sharp buzz-like noise coming from orchestra-center. Marvin's eyes scanned the shadowy figures seated in the audience. As the sound increased in volume, the patrons began to murmur. Marvin tried to speak, but couldn't open his mouth. He found it difficult to breathe. He felt his knees begin to buckle underneath him. All at once he swayed; he was about to fall onto Pamela when a stage hand appeared and caught him by the waist, preventing a complete collapse. The audience gasped and the curtain fell.

The house lights came up and brightened the auditorium. It was a full five minutes before a very large man was awakened from his snoring, escorted from his seat, and ushered to the back of the theatre and out the lobby doors.

Marvin Shay's opening night performance had been ruined. He could not go back on stage. Having someone fall asleep and interrupt the importance of his opening recitation was bone-crushing to his spirit, something he would never get over. An announcement was made. The first act would start anew and Nelson Trigget, understudy, would replace Marvin.

Nelson carried the performance to its spectacular climax amidst cheers of abandoned delight.

Later that evening, shortly before midnight, in a corner booth of a dimly-lit tavern on West 52nd Street, Marvin Shay's former understudy handed an envelope to a very large man seated across the table from him.

The man accepted the envelope from him and yawned.

Thank you for reading *Lillian on Sunday: Stories of the Human Heart*. I hope you enjoyed it. If you did, please leave a review on the site where you purchased the book.

Lightning Source UK Ltd.
Milton Keynes UK
UKHW010709290721
387974UK00003B/709